The Well-Beaten Path

A Beautiful Love Story

Handwritten inscription:

1st

To My Precious Grandson
Landon

Love always and Forever
Nana

This Book will help you see & understand
the heart of a Woman Better. And it
will improve your marriage,
when
that day
comes.

VICTORIA DEAN

Book 1 of 7 in the Gran Series

Fulton Books, Inc.
Meadville, PA

Published by Fulton Books 2021

ISBN 978-1-63860-321-4 (paperback)
ISBN 978-1-63860-322-1 (digital)

Printed in the United States of America

CHAPTER 1

For we are all on a path; some are on a well-beaten path.
There are two paths in life—one leads to peace,
and the other one leads to destruction.
Sometimes those paths collide.
Seek peace and the peacemaker.

As Sophie pulled up to the lake house, memories flooded over her. She couldn't believe it had been four years since she had been there. She was only there for two days. Gran Brewer's funeral had been that weekend. It was so painful. She loved all of her grandparents, but she was closer to Gran and Granddad Brewer. Her family loved the lake and the lake house. She had lived here from age six until she was thirteen, on this lake. The day she left the lake house at thirteen was so very painful for her. She left her best friend Jim. He was fifteen. They both cried their eyes out, and she got her first kiss. It was his first too. After he kissed her, he said, "I think we need to practice that." She turned her face up to him, and he gave her a kiss that left a vivid memory she never forgot. She was sure he was her love of a lifetime. The lake house and the sanctuary were her places of peace and comfort. Also, her best friend was here. When he was saying goodbye, they were almost back to her gran's, and it started raining. He took off his outer shirt and made her put it on. He kissed her again, and she ran back to Gran's, crying, and she kept that shirt.

His grandparents were like hers too. They welcomed her with open arms after the death of her parents and brother who died in a car accident. That was still a difficult memory for her. Her brother,

Timmy, was only four. Gran and Granddad Brewer had been watching her when her family died in the car accident. She had chicken pox and couldn't go on the trip with them. Gran and Granddad Brewer had been wonderful to her. She had a good life here. She had given her heart to Jesus at age seven and knew she would see her family again one day. Her granddad had built this lake house fifty years ago, and the little sanctuary one year later. He would go out to the lake and pray often. He said then, one day an idea came to him to build the sanctuary. He and Gran loved to walk in the early morning and evenings, so he chose that spot. It was a favorite place to look out over the lake. He used to take out a few trees to keep the view open, but they were growing up now. He was a wonderful man in every way. She missed him so much, and all of her grandparents. She had been very blessed. All of them left her with a beautiful heritage of walking with God and a financial blessing that was caring for her and Abby now.

The little sanctuary was just up and around the hill from the lake house. The path was all around the lake. The sanctuary sat on the highest place on their property. The little sanctuary was such a special place. She had gone daily for seven years, then always when she came to visit, usually every three to six months. She usually was only there one day and night and unfortunately didn't get to see her friend Jim many of those visits. She always hoped she would see him at the sanctuary. Sometimes she would walk almost to Gran Nelson's, his gran, and see if she could get a glimpse of him anywhere. That was heartbreaking to miss him almost every time. She asked about him when her granddad Brewer died six months after she moved. He was away at a sports camp. The weekend of Gran Brewer's funeral, he was visiting his other grandparents in Ohio. Sophie always called Jim's gran when she was in town, and Gran Nelson would come visit her at Gran Brewer's house. Jim would come along if he was where he could, and she always got a kiss on those occasions that they got to see each other.

After he graduated and went to college, she never got to see him again. When he was there, she wasn't. They both assumed that was just meant to be. He met Jenna his first year of college, and she was determined to get him and did. The enemy caught him and Sophie both off guard. They had grown up so close, always claiming each other's grandparents as their own. They always had tea when she came to town. It rained the day of Gran Brewer's funeral, and she was devastated. She usually went to the sanctuary every visit back to the lake house, but she didn't feel she could do it that visit. Gran had walked the path with her the last time she was here.

CHAPTER 2

After the reading of the will, Aunt Linda called and told her that Gran and Granddad Brewer had left the house and fifteen acres of prime lakefront property to her and that she had a trust fund from her parents and grandparents. She would be over it until Sophie was twenty-one. The deed was fixed, so the land could not be sold or divided unless it was to her children. It had to stay in the bloodline. Her aunt Linda had lived here until three weeks ago. She had moved to Birmingham, Alabama, to be with her daughter, who was expecting her first child. They lived in Aunt Linda's house. She and Uncle Larry bought it when he was in the military. He went on a mission seventeen years ago and didn't come back. It was very difficult for her and Avery. The lake was healing for them. They visited often and spent a lot of time here in the summer. They moved in before Gran died. She needed someone in the house with her. Then after college, Avery wanted to live in Birmingham. She and two college friends moved into their house in Birmingham. They found careers there and loved the area. Aunt Linda's daughter, Avery, married two years ago and chose to stay at the house in Birmingham. Now her mother is there too.

Aunt Linda left a lot of things that Gran had said were to be Sophie's at the lake house which was left to Sophie. Her grandparents had beautiful wood furniture. Granddad had made much of it. It was his hobby. There was a beautiful cradle in the attic. She planned to bring it down and use it. She would put it in the dining room so she could hear and see her Abby Grace as she was cooking. Abby would be making an appearance soon. Sophie had shared some of those beautiful pieces of furniture and pictures with her aunt and cousins—Avery and Emily and James. Her aunt had cared for the lake house and lived in it until Sophie was ready to move back. Her grandfather Brewer had bought her aunt Connie a house in Macon, Georgia, when she married. That's where Uncle Randy and his family moved to when he left his home in Indiana. He and Connie met in college and then he found a good job in Macon, and she agreed to move there. They had two children, Emily and James—great cousins. Her grandparents had left a trust fund for all the grandchildren. Grandfather Brewer had a career in the insurance industry and had built a billion-dollar business. He was well able to leave a good inheritance to his family, and he did. They all knew that, more importantly, he wanted them to have a rich inheritance in the heavenly realm and a great faith in Jesus. He was an amazing example. His faith was evident to all who knew him. They all loved him and Gran so very much.

Aunt Linda had the house professionally cleaned three weeks ago for Sophie when she moved. She didn't want her to have to do anything but move in and enjoy. She knew Sophie was having a baby in the coming weeks. She also knew the Nelsons and that they loved all her family and would be there for Sophie. Mrs. Nelson had asked Sophie's aunt Linda when she found out she was leaving if someone else in the family was coming to live on the lake.

"Sophie has married and is expecting, she may move back. I think she is considering it."

"That would be wonderful," Gran said. And at the same time, she felt a knot in her stomach. She would love to see Sophie and said so, yet she worried about what it would do to Jim. How he would handle it. As she talked to Granddad about it, she said, "James, I worry about what this will do to Jim."

"Well, let's pray and not mention it till we know for sure."

The timing was perfect for Aunt Linda and Sophie. As Sophie did a walk through, the memories here were sad yet precious. She had thought of coming back many times but just didn't think she could face it without them, and she was sure Jim had moved on, and the thought of seeing him with someone else was more than she could take. Oh, how she wished she had come back here when Gran Stewart had passed away. Her life would have been much different for sure. As she looked over the house, it was very clean, but she was a germaphobe. She had brought three cans of disinfectant and a mask. She sprayed everything. It had to be free of germs, especially since there would be a newborn here in seven weeks. She put her hand on her tummy and said, "Little girl, you are gonna love it here." Here was about to be greater than Sophie could have ever imagined.

CHAPTER 3

Sophie had gone to the restroom and locked the lake house. She had to be back by ten in the morning. The new furniture was coming between ten thirty and noon. Her best friends Connie and Debbie would be there by noon, and her moving van from Atlanta was to arrive between one and four o'clock. She was excited. A fresh start was what she needed. She believed it was the right decision to come back here and that God would help her. Connie and Debbie were gonna be here three days to help get her settled in. Her eyes went to the well-beaten path up the hill. She knew she shouldn't do it, but she couldn't resist the pull. It had been too long. It was time, and she didn't want to wait. She got another bottle of water from the car, keys in one pocket and a small pack of tissues and her phone in the other. She was in comfy canvas flats, so up and around the path she went. The path seemed farther than she remembered. She looked down at her tummy and knew it was the extra weight she was carrying. Tears poured down her cheeks as the little sanctuary came into view. Oh, what precious memories.

In that sanctuary is where she really learned to pray, hearing her grandparents cry out to God as they prayed for family, friends, and the needs of the world to be met. They were givers and walked with God up close and personal. She knew that place was anointed, that God's presence was felt there, and prayers answered. Out of necessity and for everyone around, Granddad had built a little restroom. No plumbing, of course, but it met needs. She stopped in. It was clean and had tissue and hand sanitizer. "Wow," said Sophie, "someone is caring for the place." As she walked to the sanctuary, approximately five hundred feet away, tears began again. She looked up into a beautiful blue sky with fluffy white clouds and said, "Granddad, you left quite a beautiful legacy, not just for our family, but for the community also." She thanked her Father in heaven for taking care of her and Abby Grace and for getting them safely back where they belonged. The weathered little sanctuary was a beautiful sight. She was sobbing brokenly as all the memories filled her. She walked inside and was amazed it was spotless and that there were tissues and a wastebasket and hand sanitizer. It was wonderful someone was caring for it too! She wondered who. Her aunt had been gone three weeks. Sophie knelt at the altar where she had prayed so many prayers through the years, and as she prayed, she began to pour out her deepest fears to the Lord. Was she gonna be all right here? Her and the baby. "Oh, Father God," she said, "help me. I can't do this alone. I need help! Send the right people into our lives, and give me strength for this part of the journey. Send angels and keep me and my baby safe." Again, she cried out, "Lord, you've got to send help. I can't do this alone or without you." She prayed for safety for Connie and Debbie as they traveled tomorrow and that all would go well with all the deliveries. Slowly she pushed up from the altar, feeling very tired and weak after all those tears, and started back down the well-beaten path, thinking, *I want to do this every day for the rest of my years. I'm going to bring my Abigail Grace and teach here to pray, and about the grace and mercy of Jesus our Lord and Savior.* And about their wonderful Christian heritage that had been passed down, and how God had blessed her family through all the years because they walked with Him and blessed others. That's why they had a rich inheritance to pass on. She was walking a path they had prepared. She was walking the path that led to everlasting life because of seeds they had sown. She wanted to be a seed sower so she too could leave a rich inheritance to Abby Grace and any other children the Lord God would give her.

CHAPTER 4

Jim was approaching the sanctuary and heard a woman weeping very brokenly. He rarely met anyone out here, and he came daily. Although he knew others used it from around the lake and came in as they walked the path around the lake. A lady named Kelly and her daughter Ahna lived down to the left in a small cottage. She cleaned houses for a living and was well-known around here as a prayer warrior and strong woman of God. He came one day, and she was cleaning the sanctuary. He told her he would pay her to clean it weekly. She was highly recommended by everyone she cleaned for. He also paid her to help Gran with spring-cleaning and again in late fall. He thought as he got a little closer, *That's not Kelly. I don't think*. He felt guilty being so close, as he was drawn closer. He wanted to know that whoever it was, she was okay. He knew the Lord sent him out here.

He heard her say, "Lord, you've got to send help. I can't do this alone or without you!" Jim backed away, and in a few minutes, she came out and started back toward the Brewer house.

Then he said, "Oh my god! Is that Sophie?" The tall thin frame and long flowing chestnut hair came into view as she started around the path. It had to be her. Before he could call out to her, he heard a scream. As she came into his sight again around the hill, he heard her say, "Oh, Jesus, send help."

Then she heard a deep emotional voice say, "I'm here," as he got down beside her. He knew it was her before he saw those beautiful emerald eyes. "Oh, Jesus," he said as his eyes saw her swollen abdomen. "Oh, Sophie, where are you hurt?"

She was speechless for a moment. "Jim," she said with relief in her voice. She was shaking and crying. Jim took out his clean white handkerchief and wiped her eyes, and she said, "Help me up first!"

"Where are you hurt?"

"Just my backside and my pride!" she said.

"Catch your breath a minute," Jim said, and he laid his hand lovingly around the front of her swollen abdomen and was relieved when he felt a strong kick. She heard him give a sigh of relief.

"Help me up, please. This ground is hard."

He put one strong arm around her back and one in front for her to pull up with. "Slow and easy," he said, and as she stood, he said, "How do you feel on your feet?" They were both clinging to each other and breathing in the wonderful scent of each other.

She thought, *Mercy, he smells good.* She said, "I'm okay," though she felt a little dizzy. His kindness was very endearing. She went to take a step and started swaying. She was in his arms immediately, and he carried her back to the sanctuary and sat down on the altar, with Sophie on his lap.

He said, "Lord, I mean no disrespect! Lord, please help Sophie and her baby. Give her strength, and I pray she nor her baby will have any ill effects from the fall. Thank you, Lord, for sending me out here at the right time! Amen."

Sophie said, "Yes, amen." All of a sudden, he realized he was holding her in a warm embrace, and she was snuggled under his chin and in his arms like she belonged there, and it sure felt like she did. Sophie was thinking, *Move girl! Get up!* But she hadn't felt this kind of safe or cared for since she was in these arms the last time, and it had been a few years. His phone rang, and they both jumped!

He said sorry. She started to get up, and he pulled her back and held his arm around her as he hit *dismiss* on the phone and looked into her beautiful face and those lovely emerald eyes. She had broken his heart when she moved away and didn't come back. He could always get lost in those eyes. He caught himself and said, "How are you feeling?"

"Like my tail is going to be very sore!"

"Are you in pain anywhere else?"

"No, I think I'm okay. Maybe a bit dehydrated after that good long cry. I dropped my water bottle when I fell. It's probably all the way down the hill."

"Are you visiting the lake house?" he asked. "And why are you out here alone and with a baby in your tummy! You should not be out here alone."

She said, "Father was with me. And he sent you to get me up!" She stood up, and he did too.

"How are you feeling on your feet?"

"A little weak and lightheaded."

"Let's sit you back down." And without a thought, he pulled her back down on his lap. She didn't resist. He pulled her head gently to his shoulder and put his arm back around her. He picked up the phone and called his gran and asked her if she would drive back to the sanctuary and bring a bottle of water.

"Jim, are you okay? Did you sprain an ankle?"

"No, Sophie is back here, and she has fallen."

"I'm on my way and praying." And she was. As she prayed for Sophie, she felt such a peace that everything was all right, although she remembered Linda said Sophie was expecting a baby. She prayed for the baby also.

Jim said to Sophie, "We probably need to call your aunt Linda and husband."

"My aunt is in Birmingham, awaiting the birth of her first grandchild, and my husband passed away two months ago in a car accident." Another flood of tears came.

"I'm sorry," he said. He pulled his hankie out of his pocket again and gently dried those beautiful eyes again, like he had done the day she left and moved to Atlanta. Gran had taught him to always carry a clean white handkerchief.

She said, "They do come in handy." He was glad she taught him that. She was right. He held it to her nose for her to blow, as he had done more than a few times in their lives. He held her and enjoyed the moments. She didn't move. It felt too good and so very right. Gran was there quick. Sophie moved beside him when she heard the car door. Gran checked her over and gave her the water. Sophie said, "When I fell, my water bottle went down the hill."

Gran said, "And you made a quick work of that bottle."

"Yes," she said, "now I need to go to the restroom."

"It's still in the same place," Gran said.

"Thanks," Sophie said as she got up. Jim was right there to help. Gran did not miss his concern, and she felt she was seeing much more. Gran walked with Sophie to the restroom and back. As they got in the car, Jim filled them in on what happened, including the overwhelming feeling that he had to come out here. And Sophie filled them in on what she was doing here. She lived at Gran Stewart's after her death, then married her husband, who died in a car accident two months ago.

Gran said, "I'm so sorry, we had no idea. Your Aunt Linda said that you were married and expecting and that you might move back she wasn't sure. We both went through a busy season, and somehow, we didn't know your husband had passed."

Sophie said, "It's been a stressful season, and I wanted to come home to the lake and raise my baby here. I wanted to give her the rich heritage I'd had."

Then they were at Grans, and she said, "Sophie, are you sure you don't need to be checked by a doctor?"

Jim said, "Do you remember Russ?"

"Of course I do," Sophie said.

"Well, he just opened his OB practice this year and is doing well."

"Great to know. I need one soon, and now I need to go to the restroom again."

"You know where it is." Jim watched her as she walked away. She had hardly changed over the years; well, maybe became even more beautiful. With fascination on his face, he looked heavenward and said, "Thank you, Lord, for bringing her back. I pray I don't lose her again." When she came out, Gran was in the kitchen making her a turkey and cheese sandwich with lettuce and tomato. Sophie didn't argue. She devoured it and a piece of banana bread and another bottle of water.

She thanked them both and said, "I need to get back to my car and the hotel."

"Rest," Gran said. "Please don't think me pushy, but, dear, you should not be alone after the fall today."

"I'm okay. I just have a sore tail which I think will be more so by tomorrow."

"Exactly. What if you wake up from a nap at the hotel and find you need to go to the restroom and can't get up? And you may fall again trying."

Sophie looked at her and said, "But I can't impose further. I ruined your afternoons."

"Nonsense," they both said. Jim would have done almost anything to keep her there.

Gran said, "Come on, let's get you in a recliner with feet up for a nap. All the other stuff can wait a couple of hours." She picked up a bell off the China cabinet.

Sophie looked at Jim over her shoulder as Gran led her away and said, "We will catch up later."

"Yes, we will," he said. Gran settled Sophie in the recliner with her shoes off and covered her with a soft blanket and said, "Ring that bell if you need anything." She felt so at ease and comfortable here as she always had. Being at the Nelsons' was just like being at her grandmother's. She always felt so loved and cared for there. Sophie was just falling asleep when the phone rang. It was Connie. She said, "Connie, let me finish my nap and I will call."

"Okay," Connie said. She could tell Sophie was very sleepy. Jim's gran had doctored as many of her boo-boos as Gran Brewer had. The two grans were great friends, and those two kids had played a lot together through the years.

CHAPTER 5

Jim felt he couldn't leave. He was afraid she would disappear out of his life again, and he felt like it would hurt worse than the first time. Gran saw his pain and came with a cup of tea for both of them. She said, "Let's sit a minute," and she pointed to the love seat, and as they sat down, she said, "Don't overthink it. God brought her back. She needs us, and He put you in the right place at the right time. He will work out this puzzle. Let Him have His way, only forge ahead with His lead." She patted his hand, and he captured hers like he had seen Granddad do time after time.

He kissed her hand and said, "Thank you, Gran. You know me so well. I love you so very much."

She said, "I love you too."

He placed his head against her shoulder and said, "You're the wisest woman I know."

"Thanks," she said. Then they finished their tea and she said, "Why don't you go pick me a few green tomatoes? I know a little lady who loves them." He leaned over and kissed her head and took their cups to the kitchen as he was going to pick tomatoes. Sophie was exhausted. She slept for two hours and fifteen minutes and only woke up then because she had to go to the restroom. She sat there a minute, thinking about what had transpired today, and it felt like she was in this house just last week.

She said, "Lord I need this, but is it okay that I just jumped back in their lives as if it was yesterday?" He has surely married and moved on. She saw pictures of him and a baby boy in the den. But it didn't feel that way when he was holding her today. She felt so ashamed that she had enjoyed being in those arms again. He was a married man! She let out a sore moan and got out of the chair. Gran and Jim both came through the door with a look of great concern. She said, "Sorry. I didn't mean to startle anyone. I'm okay. Just soreness moving in. I guess tomorrow I will have to call a wrecker to help me up."

"Maybe you should stay down a few days," Jim said.

"Nope, that wouldn't be good for me or Abigail Grace."

"Oh, Sophie, that's a beautiful name," Gran said.

"Yes, it is," Jim said. Sophie's grandmothers were Abigail and Grace, and Jim's gran was also Grace. "She will be breathtaking, like her mommy," he said.

She was caught by surprise and the way he was looking at her and said, "Oh, stop it. Shouldn't you be getting home to your family instead of worrying about me." She saw great pain fill his face. He tried to turn away. She caught his arm and said, "What's wrong? What is it?"

He broke down crying and said, "They died in a house fire fourteen months ago. I moved in here again." Gran went to check on dinner. She felt the Holy Spirit was at work here, and she needed to get out of the way. Her husband would be home soon. She called and told him what was happening and asked him to pray, which he did. Sophie put her arms around Jim, and as her baby moved against him, he cried for his nine-month-old son who died in the fire—James Micah, named after his grandfathers. He missed his son 24-7. Sophie cried with him. Gran heard the pain and grief in his voice. She cried with him as she did day after day and asked Father God to heal his pain. Maybe this was God's plan to heal them both together. Sophie held him and cried with him for at least five minutes.

"I'm so sorry," Sophie said, and he cried again. It felt so good to be held in her arms and comforted by the love of his life. He couldn't believe she was here in his arms, and he didn't ever want to let her go. He almost broke off the engagement to Jenna twice. He wished he had. He wished he had gone to find Sophie.

He pulled himself together for the second time today and said, "I'd better let you go to the restroom." She gave him a big squeeze and went.

She came out feeling better and said, "I need to get back to my car and the hotel. I've got a busy day tomorrow."

"I will help you tomorrow," he said. "I have no appointments." She looked up into those blue eyes that she had loved so much and then to his lips. He had been her first and best kiss. She realized she was staring into his face and thinking of their last kiss. She looked away, flushed and breathless. She thought, *What is going on with me? It must be raging hormones because I'm expecting.* Jim felt it to his toenails and was quite shaken. He had wanted to kiss her and might have if she kept looking at him that way. Gran didn't miss a thing and somehow felt so at peace with it. She knew only her Father could orchestrate all that had transpired today. Jim's granddad came in from work just in time.

After a wonderful dinner, Sophie said, "Can I get a ride back to my car?" They all three protested.

Gran said, "If you don't stay here tonight, I won't sleep at all."

"Nor I," Jim said.

Granddad looked at her and raised an eyebrow and said, "Three against one."

"Okay," she said. "But I must warn you that I have nightmares."

"Well, we will just have to pray," they all three said at once! She had called them Gran and Granddad since she was six and had come to live at the lake house. She and Jim had much in common since they both had lost their parents and were raised by their grandparents. Both families tried to give them both all the love they could. Growing up at the lake house had been amazing. She had felt loved, accepted, and blessed. It broke her heart when Granddad Brewer was dying, and Gran had to send her to her grandmother Stewart's so she could devote her time to caring for her sick husband. He had a stroke while mowing one day and never overcame the effects of it. Then pneumonia took him home to be with Jesus. She loved her grandmother Stewart, and she was wonderful to Sophie. And needed her. She was so lonely after her husband had died of heart failure. Sophie was a breath of fresh air in Gran Stewart's home. Living in the outskirts of Atlanta though just didn't hold a candle to living on the lake and walking to the sanctuary daily to pray. You could feel the tingles of the Spirit in that place. It felt so good to be back here. She never wanted to leave again. This place was good for her and would be for Abby Grace. She would love it also.

CHAPTER 6

After a wonderful dinner, Sophie and Gran went to get her purse from her car and her things from the hotel. Jim and Granddad sat out on the screened porch and waited. And Granddad said, "I knew something happened when you didn't come back after lunch." Jim told him about the soup spill and coming home to change his shirt and having that overwhelming feeling that he had to go to the sanctuary.

"It was God sending me there for her." Tears fell down his cheeks, and Granddad held him and cried with him. Jim said, "I couldn't leave. I was afraid she would get away again, and I don't think I could take that."

Granddad said, "Let's pray," and they did. They asked Father to be with each of them as they ministered to Sophie and her baby. When their ladies returned, they had frozen yogurt on the porch, and before bed, they all prayed and rebuked the nightmares and prayed for her soreness to go and a good night's rest for all. At seven o'clock the next morning, Gran heard her up. They came into the hall at the same time. Sophie was moving slow and sore.

Gran said, "Are you having any pain other than soreness and stiffness?"

"No," Sophie said, "and this too shall pass. But I could sure use a cup of tea."

Gran gave her a hug and said, "Me too." After breakfast, they all prayed again. Granddad had a prior commitment. The others sat around the table, and Gran asked Sophie what her day looked like.

"Busy," she said. "I need to be at the house by ten, and I need to get groceries first. The furniture will be delivered between ten thirty and noon. My friends Connie and Debbie are coming around noon to help. The truck with the things from Atlanta will be here between one and four o'clock. We hope to be mostly settled in by bedtime."

"Does the yard need mowing?" Jim asked.

"No," she said, "Aunt Linda had someone take care of it."

"Is there anything I can do for you this morning?"

"No," she said, "but now after lunch that's another thing."

"Well, how about I mow here this morning, shower, and pick up lunch for everyone. Is one o'clock good?"

The ladies both said perfect.

"And now what sounds good?" They decided on Mexican. Jim said, "Let me show you a menu." And he pulled it up on his phone.

She loved it and said, "It sounds like my kind of place."

"It's great," Jim said. "One of our favorite places." She chose something for her and the girls. Gran chose for her and Granddad. Jim said, "Do I need to get drinks and ice?"

"No," she said, "I emptied the ice maker yesterday, so the ice would be fresh, and I will get drinks and make sweet tea. What would you like to drink, sir?"

"Sweet tea for me."

Gran said, "To the potty, missy! We'd better get to the grocery store."

Sophie said, "Gran, you don't have to. I just need to get back to the lake house. You probably have plenty to do today."

Gran put her hands on Sophie's cheeks and said, "What I want to do today is spend it with you!" and they hugged. Jim was misty-eyed; they all were.

Sophie said, "It feels so good to be back here."

"We are all happy to see you back," said Gran.

Jim said, "Amen."

Gran said, "And we are so excited about meeting Abby Grace."

"Yes, we are," Jim said.

Gran grabbed muffins from the freezer and said, "We're off."

"See you ladies at one," Jim said. "Call if you need anything."

"Bring a toolbox," Sophie said over her shoulder as she and Gran were leaving.

"Will do." His heart was doing flip-flops at the sight of her this morning. Her hair was half wet still and curling around her face. Lord, she was more beautiful than he ever thought possible. He had hoped and prayed she would come back here. God had answered his prayers. He was overjoyed. As he mowed, Sophie was all he could think of. Sophie and Gran got groceries and four cases of water and were back by nine thirty. They left the water for Jim to bring in and had everything put up and had muffins and tea before the furniture delivery. Sophie knew where she wanted things. The guys from the furniture store were good and had everything in place and the washer and dryer hooked up and were out of there before the girls got there at twelve twenty-five. They loved the lake house and Gran. Sophie walked them out back to the lake. It was a beautiful day in a beautiful place.

The girls loved it there and said, "Hey, you've got room. We just might have to think of moving to the lake."

"Anytime!" Sophie said. When they got back to the house, Granddad had just arrived. Jim was behind him with lunch. He came in, and Sophie's hair was in a ponytail. She was gorgeous. The girls didn't miss that he hardly took his eyes off her. Everyone noticed. They all pigged out. Everyone was stuffed. Sophie went to the potty, and when she came out, Gran said, "Come here, little girl." She led her to the den and said, "In that recliner, little lady."

Sophie said, "I need to get the new sheets out of the dryer. And show Jim what to put together."

"The girls and I can take care of that. You rest."

"But, Gran, you need to rest too."

"Okay, I will get them started and be back." Gran kissed her on top of the head like her other two grans had always done. Two hours later, Sophie woke up. Gran and Granddad were napping in the living room. Jim and the girls were settled on the back porch, getting to know each other. Sophie heard him say to them that he might know someone who could stay with her in the afternoon and at night. And that he and Gran would check on her daily.

She stepped out on the porch and said, "It sounds like you all have me covered."

"We are trying," he said and told them about the Silva girls. "You will love them," he said. "Is it okay if I call and see if they can come tomorrow afternoon?"

"Yes," they all said. Jim couldn't get ahold of them. He left a message and told Luz he would like to talk to her about a project to help a friend.

He said, "If you are busy, we can talk after church tomorrow." The beds were made. The crib was put together, the legs and wheels were on the bassinet, and the changing table was together. Sophie was overjoyed.

She said, "You guys are the best." They heard the truck from Atlanta coming in the driveway. Sophie had brought several pieces of furniture from Gran Stewart's house—the round game table, her grandparents' rockers, and Gran's china and large crystal collection. She brought nothing to remind her of Gregory. She burned her wedding pictures. She brought a bookcase with special books, games, and her grandparents' Bibles, a hope chest full of tablecloths and two beautiful tea sets. She also had Gran Brewer's tea set that matched her china. She was so blessed to be taken care of so wonderfully by her grandparents and to have such godly examples all of her life. Granddad took the girls to town at five thirty. Gran, Jim, and Sophie sat and discussed what was left to do. Jim helped her hang pictures. Gran was making more tea.

Jim turned and saw Sophie on the step stool and yelled, "Sophie, what are you doing?" as he made a dash for her. She burst into tears. He caught her hand and said, "Come down from there," and she was crying her eyes out. He held her and said, "I'm sorry I yelled, angel. You scared me. You could have fallen again. We can't have that." She cried several minutes. He said, "Please forgive me. I guess I scared you enough to cause you to fall. I never want to see you hurt ever again. I will help you with anything anytime. Just ask, okay? Please stay safe and off of ladders and step stools, okay?" She nodded against his shoulder, and he took out his handkerchief and dried her eyes and held it to her nose for her to blow.

She laughed and said, "I don't know how you have put up with this crybaby and all those dirty handkerchiefs."

He said, "That's what friends are for."

She gave him a heart-melting smile and said, "I've got to go wash my face before they get back."

"Yes," he said, "they will beat me up if they know I made you cry. I'm really sorry, you just scared me."

"Sorry," she said and went and washed her face. Ten minutes, and they came back with dinner. After dinner, the Nelsons prayed with the girls. All the furniture was in place, so they went home. After insisting that the girls let them bring lunch after church tomorrow, Sophie said, "You are spoiling me too much."

"Nonsense," they said as they left for the evening. Everyone had worked hard and was ready for showers and bed.

CHAPTER 7

The girls were 80 percent done Saturday night. Gran had invited them to church. They declined and said they were going to watch their church online but would visit next week. Sophie said, "I will miss my church, but God has one here for me. I will find it." She promised to go to Gran's church the next week. The girls all showered, got in their pj's, and Connie and Debbie wanted to know all about the handsome hunk.

"He was your first love?"

"Yes!" she said. "And my first kiss! When I had to move, we both cried."

"Why is a sweet, gentle, godly man like him not married?" Connie said.

"He was, and he had a son with her, but when the baby was nine months old, the house burned and his wife and son died in the fire, while Jim was working out of town for a couple of days."

"That's horrible. It had to be so painful for him."

"Yes, and still is."

"Well, I think I want him to be your love you grow old with," Connie said.

"I agree," said Debbie. "And the way he looks at you. We think he wants to be."

"Let's slow down and see what the Lord's plan is," Sophie said.

"Well, we're just saying it looks like you're in good hands here. But if you had not lived in Atlanta, we would have missed a great friend. It's plain to see you belong here. It's not so far. We can visit often."

"We will see, you two! I think you two need to move here and find your forever loves."

"Sounds like a plan," Debbie said. "We will check it out next weekend." After breakfast Sunday morning, they watched church online.

Then Sophie said, "I have to show you my special place."

"The sanctuary?" they both said in unison.

"Yes," she said.

"Sophie, are you sure that you're up to that? You just fell two days ago."

"Yes!" Sophie said. "And I need to get this soreness out!" She had keys in one pocket, and phone and hanky in the other, and they each had a bottle of water. Halfway up the hill, she was having second thoughts.

Connie said, "Are you okay?" as Sophie paused.

"Yes, but I'm so sore. I need this."

"Okay," Connie said.

Debbie said, "Maybe we should wait till tomorrow."

"Let's press on, girls." They crested the hill. They fell in love with the little sanctuary.

"It's beautiful," they said. They went in and prayed. They had to help Sophie up. She was in pain when she knelt down, and getting up was a three-person job. They got on each side and pulled her up.

She said, "Don't say a word about this. I will be fine." They both were concerned about her walking back down the trail. She said, "I'm okay, I will be careful." They were back at the house before Jim and his grandparents came with lunch.

He said, "Should I ask if Mrs. Silva and her daughters can come at three thirty?"

"Yes," she said, "that would be perfect."

"Well, you grab a quick nap. We will come also. Gran is bringing dessert." The Silva family had worked for the Nelsons for over twenty years. Armando, his lovely wife, Luz, daughters, Karen and Anna, and sons, Joel and Mariano. Sophie and the girls loved Luz and her daughters. They made an agreement that Anna would stay daily until school started back in a week. Then she would stay until six after school. Karen would come at three o'clock Monday, when the girls left for Atlanta. Then Karen would come every evening at six and spend the night. Anna couldn't come on Tuesday morning. She had a dentist appointment and had to get new shoes for school. She would be here in the afternoon.

Gran said, "I can come Tuesday morning."

Sophie started to say no but realized she needed to tell Gran her story soon.

Jim said, "I'd love to take your boxes to the girls' younger brothers if that's okay with you, Mrs. Silva."

"You know those boys well. Thank you."

"I will help you load them," Granddad said.

Jim turned to Sophie and asked if she needed anything done before he left. She said at the moment she couldn't think of anything. "I will call tomorrow if that's okay."

"Sure," she said. Everyone said their goodbyes and wished the girls a safe trip back home the next day. Sophie knew she would miss them, and was happy they were coming again next weekend. By the time the girls were ready to leave, all of Abby Grace's clothes were washed and in her chest. Her bed was ready, bassinet, and changing table. Diapers were in her diaper stacker hanging on the end of the crib, and wipes on one side. The changing table had wipes and diapers.

"It looks like a baby is coming," they all said. They took pictures of the three of them in the nursery and lots of pictures of Sophie, good tummy shots for Abby to see later. Those thoughtful girls had also taken pictures of Jim putting everything together. He was so careful with his work he never even knew they were taking them. Sophie and the girls washed all of Abby's furniture and put sheets on it all—crib, changing table, and bassinet. They covered it all with clean dust sheets to keep the dust off. Jim called at four thirty on Monday to make sure Karen was there and all was well.

"Do you want to walk with me down to the lake later?" he asked.

"Sure, I'd love to," she said. They kept the conversation light and away from anything personal. When Karen came out, he talked with her a few minutes, and it helped them get to know each other better before leaving.

He said, "Would you like to walk again tomorrow evening, maybe seven?

"Yes," she said, "I'd love to." He leaned toward her, and her heart skipped a beat.

He kissed her forehead and said, "Call me anytime if you need anything."

She nodded and smiled and thought, *Oh boy. My emotions are out of hand.*

As he drove away, he said to himself, *Slow down, Jim! You're moving too fast.*

CHAPTER 8

Gran came at eight fifteen. She knew Sophie was an early riser. They both got a cup of tea and went to the den. Sophie began and said, "Gran, I've jumped back into your lives and bombarded you with a lot of work and busyness, and that was not the way I planned it. There has been a lot happening in my life since I left here. I'd like to share that with you."

"Okay," Gran said, "we have all the time in the world." Sophie opened her heart and mouth and shared her pain with this lady she had loved and respected all her life.

She said, "When Gran Stewart passed away unexpectedly with a stroke, I was devastated at first I couldn't function. I thought I would have many more years with her. I didn't want to touch anything. I'd get up feeling lost every day and would walk from room to room. I couldn't seem to figure out what to do next. I'd walk into the kitchen or her bedroom, and I would fall apart. It was just too sudden. With my other grandparents on dad's side, I had time to adjust to the fact they were in ill health and would pass soon. I finally decided I needed to clean out her personal things that I wasn't going to keep. There were many things that would be useful to someone else. Connie and Debbie helped me. I put a For Sale sign on her car. And pulled it out to the street the next morning. A seemingly kind young man named Gregory came and checked it out. He hung around a long time, asking questions about the car. If there were other items I was selling. 'No,' I said. He test-drove the car. He assured her the car was perfect for his younger brother, Kyle." Sophie continued to tell Gran the story.

He said, "If you will take the sign off, I will be back at noontime tomorrow with the money."

"Okay," she said.

As she reached for the sign, he took her hand and said, "I'm so sorry for your loss. I feel your pain. My grandfather passed six months ago. I understand how you feel." Then he said, "Have a good evening," and left, saying, "Till tomorrow."

"He was handsome and charming. I was lonely. It had been almost a year since I had dated anyone. The last boyfriend's job took him to Chicago, and I realized I wasn't going. I liked him, he was a great guy, we were great friends, but I didn't love him," Sophie said to Gran.

Then the next day, when Gregory came to pick up the car, he asked Sophie to dinner Friday night, and he pursued her with praise, flattery, and nice dinners. Connie and Debbie were not comfortable with him. They told her they didn't feel good about them marrying in just eight weeks. He was rushing her, but the attention felt good, so she did marry him quickly and lived to regret it. She paid for the wedding chapel. Plus, their very expensive honeymoon, that she paid way too much for, was a big disappointment. He had said there was a wonderful place in Florida he wanted to take her to. He really worked hard to convince her they should go. He was still waiting on inheritance money from his grandfather's will, and he could pay her back if they could go. It was a lie. He drank a lot daily, which was a side of him she never saw before. He wasn't nice at all when he was drinking. He said, "It's what people do on their honeymoon." She saw several new sides of him on the honeymoon, which cost her a fortune, and she was more than glad to get home. They were miserable together as soon as they got back. He started being all charming again, and he insisted they share checking accounts since they were married. He said, "That's what everyone does when they marry." She wasn't comfortable with the idea but let him talk her into it.

Two weeks later, he took her out to dinner. Then he wanted to go to the movies, then to get ice cream. He said, "We've not done anything since our honeymoon." And when they came home, they had been robbed. All of her grandmother's jewelry was gone, some expensive paintings, clocks, and her grandmother's Hummel collection, which was worth a lot. They were up for hours as the police did the report. It took forever, and they tried to lift fingerprints from everything. Sophie cried and cried. Gregory comforted her and put up a good show of being a caring husband. He apparently had plenty of practice—the house was torn apart. Sophie was devastated.

She said, "I'm afraid to stay here."

He said, "Well, thieves don't come back to the crime scene." They cleaned them out, but all he lost was a pair of diamond cuff links. Sophie almost never went to sleep. He talked her into a glass of wine. He said, "Sophie, I have to be at the office early." When she got up the next morning after only four hours of sleep, he was leaving and said he was sorry he had to leave her with all the insurance claims to handle. He had an important client this morning. She called the girls. It was Saturday morning, and they came and helped. They were both suspicious. They helped her get everything cleaned and put back. It would have taken several people, the police said, with as big a job as it was.

Connie said, "Don't you find that suspicious? You know his friends are rough characters."

I did think of that as odd," Sophie said. "It's the first time he has taken me out since our honeymoon, and we conveniently get robbed." Sophie had not fully trusted him, so she had never told him about the lake house, or her trust fund. She had never touched any of the paperwork. It was not in the house. She had a safety deposit box he knew nothing of. She said he was so torn up. "I can't believe he had a part in this, he was so sweet." But they were not buying it. The police got two sets of prints. The two teenagers were set up, but they couldn't tell or wouldn't tell the police anything helpful. The police were not satisfied that those two boys did that job by themselves. They each had $200 on them.

The next week, $500 came out of the checking account, and the house insurance would be coming out next week, so she brought it up, and he said, "I put money in that account too!"

"And you spend it all," she said.

He said, "My car insurance was due, the money was there, so I just paid it. I will put more in the account Friday." But he only put $150 in the account. She was concerned. Then the next week, her diamond earrings were gone. He made a big show of trying to help her find them, and she was sure he had taken them. She accused him. They had a fight, and he left. Then he came in very drunk and treated her very badly. They got in another big fight. She told him to leave. He hit her and said, "We are married. I live here now, and you just need to be quiet and get used to it." She told him if he didn't leave, she would call the police. He shoved her down and said, "You'd better never call the police on me or you will live to regret it." The way he looked at her scared her, and he left very angry. He didn't come back. She went to the bank first thing the next morning to take him off her account. He had already cleaned it out. She was fortunate enough to get in with her lawyer that day and file for a divorce and restraining order and to petition to change her name back to her maiden name. She had called Gregory and told him he needed to go get his stuff before five o'clock or it would be on the front sidewalk. He said a lot of degrading things to her. She didn't go home until seven o'clock. Debbie went with her in case he was still there. They locked and bolted the doors and checked the house over. He took his stuff and had made a terrible mess all through the house. He had searched through everything as if he was looking for money. Debbie spent the night.

CHAPTER 9

Sophie had a locksmith in the next day, and all the locks were changed. Three weeks later, as she returned home from work and having dinner at Connie's, she was raped as she was getting out of her car. The rapist was in the garage. When she arrived home, he was hidden beside the freezer. As she told the story, she started crying. Gran held her and said, "You have been through so much. I'm so thankful God has sustained you and brought you back here where you are safe and loved."

"Me too," Sophie said. "It gets worse. When I threw Gregory out, I threw away my birth control pills. The man who raped me is Abby's father. I'm glad. I would rather it be him. I'd be concerned having a baby by Gregory knowing now who he was. I have known Abby's father for years. Ben. He is a good, godly man."

Gran said, "I don't understand?"

Sophie said, "We went to high school together, hung out with some of the same people, went to church together. He was two years older. There was nothing ever between us. We were just friends. After high school, he went into the army and to Afghanistan. He sustained a brain injury there and doesn't comprehend much anymore. He lives with his mother and sister two streets over. I guess when he got out of the house and wandered off and saw Gran's house, it was familiar, but the doors were locked, and no one was home, so he hid in the garage. He had not seen me in two years, maybe he didn't know it was me. I tried to talk him down and get away from him, but it didn't work. He ran after he raped me. I called and had the police pick him up and take him home. I went to a local judge the next morning who was friends with my grandmother, and we handled it quietly. He was put on medicine and now he wears an ankle bracelet. I had a tall fence put around his mother's house, and mine with an automatic gate, so he was safe and others around him also, and I felt safe. I wasn't thrilled when I found out I was expecting, but I know God creates every soul, and apparently, she was meant to be born. Once I felt her move, I was in love. God had created life in me."

"That's beautiful," Gran said.

"I was really glad when I found out the baby was a girl. I think it would have been more difficult otherwise," Sophie said.

"I understand that," Gran said.

"I've got to go potty and blow my nose," Sophie said. "I will be right back. There is more!"

Gran prayed for her. Sophie came back, and Gran asked, "Does Abby's dad or family know about her?"

"No," Sophie said. "It would be painful for them, and they would want to be part of her life, and that would be difficult for me."

Gran said, "Sophie, you have such a beautiful heart, and you have experienced so much pain. You will be safe here. We will all help you and Abby Grace."

"Thank you so much. I've missed you all, and I needed a safe place to raise my baby," Sophie said. She had never thought about what Gregory would think if he found out she was expecting. One of his friends saw her out at the mall and told him! She was five months at the time. As she came in from work one day, she didn't see Gregory, but he was apparently hidden behind the bushes in the neighbor's yard. He had jumped through the gate as it was closing. She had gotten out of her car with her tote bag from school and her purse. He grabbed her and spun her around.

She screamed, and he put his hand over her mouth and said, "You'd better not do that again."

"What are you doing here?" she said. "Get out and never step foot on this property again." She pushed the button to open the gate and said to him, "Get out now!"

He said, "Whose baby are you carrying? And don't you dare say it's mine!"

"It's not," she said, and he slapped her through the face and said, "Well, you are about to get rid of it! It's not about to carry my name! I'm not about to support a baby that's not mine!" and he was trying to drag her toward the street. She was trying to get away.

She said, "I went back to my maiden name. Turn me loose now." The neighbor saw what was happening and called the police.

He heard the neighbor yell, "Turn her loose! I've called the police!"

She was crying again, so hard she couldn't talk. Gran was holding her and praying. She pulled herself together and continued, "He heard the police and shoved me down. I'm thankful Abby was okay."

"Me too," Gran said.

"As he made a run for it, his car was in the neighbor's driveway. I had not noticed it when I came home. He was trying to outrun the police, lost control of the car in a curve, and hit a tree head-on and died at the scene. I could not live there anymore. I stayed with Connie until I came here. It took me weeks to be able to go back in the house. I took both the girls and an off-duty police officer when I did go back. I didn't trust that one of his friends might decide to harm me. The house is clean and empty and on the market now. I'm blessed that my grandparents left me a house, legacy, and trust fund so Abigail Grace and I will be okay. I feel so safe here. I'm not having to look over my shoulder anymore."

Gran held her and asked, "Does Jim know any of this?"

"No, not yet," Sophie said. "I will tell him over the next few days. It's going to be hard to do." Gran prayed for her and Abby, that all things would work together for good for them.

"Romans 8:28," Sophie said, "my life verse."

Gran said, "You do feel safe here, don't you?"

"Yes," Sophie said, "I do."

"You have our blessing and help."

"Thank you, Gran. I am so thankful for you and all your help."

"I'm here anytime you need me, little lady." "Oh," Gran said, "I brought you a gift. I made you a couple of large baby quilts for Abby Grace. As she grows, the receiving blankets get too small quickly, and cold weather is coming soon."

Sophie gave Gran another hug and said, "It's so good to be back home and have a gran again."

"It's so good to have you back home again."

"Forever this time," Sophie said.

Gran said, "You and Jim both got a counterfeit love. Now you have the real thing. Grab hold and don't let go."

Sophie said, "I don't deserve him."

"Nonsense," Gran said. "Make him a happy man and say yes when he asks. He will be good to you and Abby."

"I know," she said. "He is a wonderful person, always has been." Sophie kissed Gran's cheek and said, "I'd kiss your feet if I could." They hugged, and Sophie's stomach growled.

Gran said, "I hear a hungry tummy. Come on, I know where the baby wants to eat." Sophie laughed and followed. Gran took her to a wonderful tearoom. They had a great lunch, and Gran dropped her back at the lake house.

CHAPTER 10

When Jim came that evening to walk on the side of the lake after dinner, they invited Karen to join them. She said, "You two go ahead, I need to study." As they walked, they kept the conversation light. It was a beautiful evening, with a perfect breeze coming off the lake. As they walked, just making small talk back to the house, he asked if she was feeling settled and content.

"Yes," she said, "I'm glad I came back here."

"Me too," he said. "It's good to have my old friend back again. I've missed you. I miss Granddad and Gran Brewer. They loved me and treated me like I was theirs."

"I know," she said, "we were both blessed with the best of grandparents. We had it great growing up here like we did. I wish so much that I could have stayed."

"Me too," he said. He took her hand and asked, "Do you want to walk again tomorrow?"

"Yes," she said, "I want to walk up to the sanctuary. I don't want you to think you have to watch over me. I jumped back into your life, but I don't want you to feel responsible for me."

He chuckled and said, "I just want to be seen walking with that beautiful lady with the beautiful chestnut hair that the sun dances off of."

"Oh, what a charmer you are," she said playfully. "This lady is getting so big I feel like a cow!"

"Well, I've never seen a beautiful emerald-eyed cow before."

"Ha ha," she said. "Seven tomorrow?"

"It's a date," he said. Her face clouded, and a few tears escaped. He gently brushed them away and said, "Sophie, I'm not sure you should go back up there right now." She saw he was concerned, and it touched her heart.

She said, "I need to."

He said, "I'm your friend, and I don't want to be overbearing, but I'm worried about you."

She pulled his hand to her lips and kissed the top of it and said, "You are my dear precious friend, and you are not overbearing. Tomorrow we walk to the sanctuary." He smiled and leaned forward. Her heart caught in her throat as he kissed her cheek ever so softly and paused a moment to breathe in the scent of her. She was wearing vanilla, and whatever he was wearing had her attention.

He said in an emotional husky voice, "Good night, Sophie," and kissed her hand. He watched until she was safely inside and prayed over her and Karen, her home, and Abby Grace. She went inside dreading what she had to tell him the next day and remembering how wonderful she felt and how safe she felt around him. When she went to bed, she asked Jesus to cover her. Sophie had trouble going to sleep. She did so dread telling Jim what had been happening in her life over the last few years. It was going to be difficult and painful. The chemistry between them was very obvious. They both still had feelings for each other, but would he still after she tells him how foolish she has been? She was so ashamed. What would he think of her now? She dreaded finding out, but the sooner the better.

Sophie prayed and said, "Lord Jesus, you know me and the mess I've made of my life. Please forgive me, and help Jim also." She finally got comfortable and slept after a talk with Father.

CHAPTER 11

Sophie was awakened to sounds of someone trying to get in the house. Her heart was pounding. She prayed and turned on her bathroom light and closed her bedroom door and locked it behind her so whoever was trying to get in her back door would think she was in there. She went into Karen's room and locked the door. "Karen," said Sophie.

"Yes," Karen whispered.

"Be real quiet, don't move." She put the desk chair under and against the bottom of the doorknob. Karen's heart was pounding as was Sophie's. She said, "Karen, get in the closet with me. Someone is trying to get in. You quietly call Jim." She called 911. She had a can of disinfectant spray. She was gonna go for the eyes. There was also a big umbrella—she could use the point as a weapon. She put a blanket off the closet shelf in front of the bottom of the door so if they came down the hallway, they couldn't see the light from the phone. She prayed, and someone was trying to break the door open when she heard horns blowing loud, and gunshots. She and Karen were hugging each other and praying. It seemed like forever, long terrifying minutes before they heard other sounds—people running, gunshots fired, then finally, sirens, more shots. They couldn't imagine what all was going on outside or who would be trying to get in. Karen had never been so scared in her life. Then quiet footsteps.

CHAPTER 12

When Jim got back from Sophie's, Granddad and Gran were at the kitchen table, just finishing their yogurt snack. His face said he needed to talk. Granddad pushed out a chair and said, "What's on your mind?" He looked like he was about to cry.

He said, "I feel like I just left the other side of me and it hurts. I want to be there to protect her. I love her. I always have."

Granddad and Gran both said, "We know. Have you told her?"

He said, "I'm afraid to. I'm afraid I will scare her away. I don't know what she has been through, but it had to be bad."

"Trust God to lead, and his timing," Gran said.

Granddad said, "Jim, you two were meant to be together. You both know it. Let God lead you like your Gran said." They joined hands and prayed. Granddad said, "You have our blessing. You were meant to be a dad, and there's a baby that needs one. I think the Lord is in this." Tears poured around the table, and Gran slipped away and came back and opened Jim's hand and put something in it. He looked down to see a beautiful diamond ring. He looked at Gran's hand and realized it wasn't hers.

She said, "It was your mother's."

He said, "You didn't offer it when I married Jenna."

She said, "I couldn't. I didn't feel like she was the one."

He said, "Thank you, Gran." He took her hands in his and kissed them. Tears began to pour around the table again. Then the phone rang. It was Karen. Jim was stricken with fear.

"Karen, what's wrong?"

"Someone is breaking in!"

"I'm on the way! Granddad, get two shotguns and ammo quick! Gran, call 911! Someone is breaking in at Sophie's. Go lock yourself in the bedroom and get in the closet with your pistol." They were out of the house in ninety seconds. They shot the tires on the pickup truck outside the driveway to Sophie's. They came into the driveway sideways, blowing the horn. Jim was driving, and Granddad was firing into the ground. Jim said, "Get down, Granddad, and cover me!" They had the flashers going. Jim said, "I've got to distract them." The guys ran out of the back when they heard shooting and horns. Jim was praying "Father, please send angels and protect us all." Gran and Granddad and the girls were all praying the same. Jim and Granddad fired a few bullets. Jim went to Karen's window and said, "Karen, are you okay?" No answer. He eased around back, and the hallway door from the screened porch was open. He took off his shoes and went in. He found no one. He was calling, "Sophie and Karen, are you here?"

The cops were in the driveway and said to Granddad, "We've got the prowlers." He called Jim.

Jim said, "Girls, come out. It's safe now." Granddad called Gran as he came in, saying, "Is everyone okay?" The door opened to Karen's room, and both of them were in Jim's arms, crying and saying thank you. The police sergeant said to Granddad, "That was a good idea shooting the tires."

Granddad said, "I wanted them caught. If we just scared them away, they might come back." The police took statements, fingerprinted the back porch, hallway door, and bedroom doors. Sgt. Thomas said, "The three boys are from Marietta. They said they thought the house was vacant and just wanted a place to sleep. They thought it was the house of one of the boy's cousins and they were in Florida, so they were going to stay a few days and fish."

"She used to keep a key on the back porch," the one boy said, "and we couldn't find it. We didn't know anyone was here."

Granddad said, "They are lying. They wouldn't have parked out at the road if that were true."

"I figured that out," the sergeant said. We will book them for home invasion, trespassing, and property damage, and run background checks. I will let you know something tomorrow."

Jim said, "Come on, girls, grab your stuff, and let's go." They were ready to get out of there. Karen called her parents, and they came to Gran's to pick her up. Gran was so glad to see them. They all circled and prayed and thanked God that no one was hurt and asked the Lord to give them all a good night's rest. They all had a cup of milk, some cookies and then went to bed. Before Sophie went down the hall to the guest room, Jim opened his arms, and she shyly went into them. He held her and said, "Life has been rough on you since you came back here, but it's going to get better. We are going to protect you."

She squeezed him and said, "Thank you."

He kissed the top of her head and said, "Go crawl up in Jesus's lap and sleep sweet."

"I will," she said, and they all had a good night's sleep.

The Lord watches over the path of the Godly, but the path of the wicked leads to destruction.

—Psalm 1:6 NLT

CHAPTER 13

By morning, there was bad news. Those boys had a rap sheet. Sgt. McKinny wanted to talk to Sophie to see if she knew them. He said, "It was odd they were up here breaking in." She didn't know the faces or names till she saw that last picture, and her face went white.

Jim said, "You know him."

"I know him," she said. He is Rodney, my ex-husband's best friend. I was afraid they might blame me for his death."

"Why would they do that?" asked Sgt. McKinny.

"We were fighting the day he died; he had attacked me in the driveway of my home." She was crying. Jim came to her and pulled out his white handkerchief, handed it to her, and massaged her shoulders gently. She was shaking. She calmed and said, "I told him to leave but he wouldn't. He wanted me to go with him. I was trying to get away. The neighbor even yelled and told him to turn me loose. That's when she had called the police. He was still dragging me toward the street when he heard the sirens, shoved me down, and ran. He pulled out in front of one police car, and it began to pursue him. The other stopped to help me. Gregory lost control in a curve and hit a big tree head-on; he was pronounced dead at the scene. They blame me, I guess. They must have followed my friends up on the weekend. He has several shady friends, I don't know them all. Also, our house was broken into two weeks after we came back from our honeymoon. Thousands of dollars of stuff was stolen, then a few weeks later, my diamond earrings my grandmother gave me when I graduated. My husband made a big show of trying to help me find them, but I suspected he had taken them. We got into a big fight, and he left. When he came back, he was drinking heavily and became very abusive. After that, I made him leave. He cleaned out my bank account that night. So he wasn't a good man. After he died, I found out he had married and robbed three other women. He and his friends pick up street kids and let them take the fall. They are not nice guys." Sophie looked toward their photos and said, "Today could have been much worse if I had not heard them in time. If Jim and Granddad had not been close and quick." She was shaken to the core by that thought, and so was Jim. Jim asked the sergeant if he could take her to his grandparents' to rest.

He said, "Of course."

Jim replied, "That's where we'll be if you have more questions." Sophie cried most of the way back to Gran's. Jim was holding her hand, aching for what she was going through, then suddenly he felt her stiffen.

She said, "Oh my god. Connie and Debbie may not be okay." Before he could speak, she was calling. Connie answered, and Sophie said, "Oh, thank God you are okay. Aren't you?"

"Yes," she said. "What's wrong?"

Sophie replied, "Karen and I were broken in on last night."

Connie said, "Oh Lord, are you both okay?"

Sophie replied, "Yes, apparently it was Gregory's friends."

Connie said, "Oh no, they must have followed us up there."

Sophie replied, "Yes, and that means they were watching you. Is Debbie okay? Have you talked to her today?"

Connie said, "Yes, and it was just an hour ago. Are you safe?"

"Yes, I'm with Jim. We're just leaving the police station and going to his grandparents'."

"Stay there please."

"You and Debbie stay safe," Sophie said.

"We will, I promise. You do the same, okay?" Connie went to her mother's, who was always driving her crazy trying to fix her up with all kinds of stuffy guys. Her mother worked at a large law firm and knew who was single. Connie, on the other hand, believed love happened without being set up. Her love was out there somewhere. There were several nice guys at Jim's church when they visited. She was looking forward to seeing them again at the wedding. Maybe she would catch someone's eye in her new dress and a nice hairdo. In the evening, she called Debbie, who was at her cousin Rebekah's house, who lived forty-five minutes away. They were followed by police in unmarked cars, to make sure they were not followed. It made Sophie feel better. She begged them to be careful everywhere they went and to keep their eyes on their surroundings.

CHAPTER 14

Sophie was dreading sharing her past and mistakes with Jim. She felt his love, and knew he needed to know, and soon. She prayed for God to give her the right words and the strength to say them. She knew she wanted to do it at the sanctuary. They had both been through so much pain. She felt like she wanted to spend the rest of her life loving him. She wanted the kind of lifelong love she saw in her grandparents, and his. She asked Father God if he would bless them, forgive her mistakes, and give her a good marriage. She knew Jim and knew he would be a wonderful father to Abby. She prayed for Jim. As they were driving back to Gran's, she said, "Jim, there are many things I need to talk to you about." He reached over and took her hand again.

He said, "But it can wait." He squeezed her hand and said, "You need lunch and a nap. We can talk later."

She said, "I would like to talk at the sanctuary. Can we walk back there after dinner when it's cooler? How about seven o'clock?"

"Sounds great," he said. After dinner, she got them both a bottle of water. Jim said, "Are you sure you're up to this?" She took his hand and started walking. She had a handful of paper towels. He said, "You've had an upsetting day today. Have I upset you?"

She reached and caught his face in her hands and said, "You wonderful, wonderful man of God. You have not upset me. I need to talk with you about some things, and the sanctuary is where I want to do it."

"But I'm worried about you."

"Don't be. I will be fine." Then she took his hand and led him to the well-beaten path on his grandparents' property. She asked, "Do you come to the sanctuary often?"

He said, "Once or twice a day. I would not have made it through my son's death without this place. The day you fell, I had been out here that morning. Later, I was at a business luncheon and spilled soup on my shirt. Do you remember me telling you and Gran I heard you crying so brokenly, and I was concerned? It wasn't an ordinary cry. It was a desperate one. I know Kelly, who cleans the sanctuary and restroom, comes out here, and others around the lake stop in to pray. I didn't know who was in there. I backed away to give them privacy, but I felt I should stay away from where I was. I saw you as you started back toward your grandparents' home. When I saw the tall lady with the beautiful chestnut hair dancing in the sun, I knew it was you. Before I could call out to you, I heard you scream. God sent me here for you." Her eyes fell on the little sanctuary. She fell apart, crying her eyes out. Jim held out his arms, and she walked into them. He held her and prayed out loud over her and Abby Grace. He could feel Abby moving, stirring inside Sophie, and he thought, *I want to be a part of this baby's life. I want to be her father and teach her about her heavenly Father.* She and Abby needed him as much as he needed them. He sure hoped so. As he held her in his arms, he breathed in the scent of her hair, and strong protective feelings stirred in him. She felt his love and affection. His strength of character. She knew she wanted to walk into these arms every day for the rest of her life.

She stayed a few minutes, then slowly pulled away and said, "I'm sorry, I drowned your shirt."

He leaned in and whispered, "It's available to you anytime."

"Thank you," she said. As they walked into the sanctuary, she thought, *I can trust him, and I believe he can handle what he is getting into.* She calmed.

He said, "Sophie, is something wrong with the baby?"

"No," she said. She took his hand and pulled him forward. As she got to the altar, she bowed and began crying again. He knelt beside her and prayed the Lord would help her with whatever she was dealing with. In a few minutes, she leaned back, still on her knees, and he did too.

He looked her in the face and said, "Sophie, whatever you are going through, I want to walk through it with you and help you."

She said, "I'd like that, but I need to tell you some things."

"Okay," he said, and she poured it all out and looked up into those wonderful blue eyes she loved so much.

She said, "Can you love someone like me, who has made so many mistakes?"

He said, "From now through all of eternity," and their lips met. When he pulled back, he said, "I'm so glad God brought you back to me. I've missed you so very much. I have messed up too. The woman I married and thought I loved was only playing me, and playing church to get me. Our marriage wasn't good from the beginning. It was all about the money for her. There was one of her old boyfriends in the bed with her when the house burned. I was thought to be a MURDERER for a few hours. The spouse is usually the suspect. Thank God I had an airtight alibi. The other guy's girlfriend was the one who set the house on fire." He fell apart, crying for his son.

She said, "I'm so sorry for what you've been through."

He said, "We've both been through the fire." He held her and said, "Whatever the rest of our lives hold, can we walk it together with God hand in hand?"

"Yes," she said. He had cried more than her as she told her story. She said, "I should have come back here when Gran Stewart died. I wish I had!"

"Me too," he said.

She said, "I've always belonged here. This was where the other half of me was. Now I'm back with a baby!"

"Our baby," he said. He kissed her. They both felt such a love for each other. He said, "Marry me now before Abby Grace is born, and my name will be on her birth certificate."

She said, "What will people say?"

"It doesn't matter. Marry me."

"Okay," she said. He kissed her again. They both felt their hearts would burst!

"To love and be loved is such a beautiful thing."

She said, "You have to marry me here!"

"Okay. When?" he said.

She said, "Saturday after next."

"Okay. It's a date," he said.

"Will you help me up?" she asked.

"I will," he said, "but first I have something for you." He pulled the ring out of his pocket and put it on her finger. It fit perfectly.

"It's beautiful," she said.

"It was my mother's," he said. "If you'd like another, we will go get any one you'd like."

"No, I'm honored to wear this ring. I have a question, why did your Jenna not have it?"

He told her what Gran had said, and he told her, "I didn't know she had it till last night." Then, he said, "Should I call Gran to drive back here and get us? You've had a tiring, stressful day."

"No," she said. "After I go to the restroom, you shall walk me back to Gran's."

"Drink some water first," he said as he opened up a bottle for each of them. He said, "I think we both dehydrated ourselves."

She said, "Yes, but it feels good to have that boulder off my shoulders."

He said, "Amen. Mine are lighter too." He leaned in and kissed her till her toes curled, and said, "I love you so much. It hurts every time I have to walk away from you."

"Same here," she said. And she pulled his face back to hers and kissed him like she had never kissed anyone.

He said, "Will you kiss me like that forever?"

"I will," she said. "You were my first kiss, my best kiss, and I want you to be my last kiss."

He said, "Amen. I didn't know it was possible to love anyone so deeply, except the love I had for my son. He was incredible. Lord, I loved that baby." He had another good cry. He said, "I didn't think you were coming back. I should have come after you, but I was afraid to."

She said, "I always wanted you to."

He said, "I'm sorry I didn't."

"Me too," she said.

He said, "We were made for each other."

"Amen," she said. Their hearts were light and joyful. When they got back to Gran's, they sat on the porch and talked and planned how to put together a quick wedding and reception. She said, "If we can have the reception here at your Gran's, we can drive back to the sanctuary."

"Sounds like a plan," Jim said. They called Granddad and Gran out on the porch and told them their plans.

Gran said, "Of course we can do the reception here." They had a large wonderful back deck that would be perfect.

Sophie said, "Let's keep it all simple." Connie and Debbie won't get to help much, but they were all so excited when Sophie and Jim called.

CHAPTER 15

Sophie called and checked on Karen before it got late and told her Jim had asked her to marry him. She said yes and that she wouldn't be ready to go back home until she and Jim married. She never wanted to risk her or her sister being hurt. Karen congratulated her and said, "Do you want to tell mom?"

"Yes, I'd love to," Sophie said. She told Luz again that she was so sorry. That she would never knowingly put her girls in danger. She said, "We are going to need all of you helping to get this wedding finished."

"You can count on us all," Luz said.

"Thank you," Sophie said. "We are keeping it simple and marrying at the sanctuary."

"That's perfect," Luz said. "We will help in any way we can."

"Thank you," Sophie said. "You are all so kind." They were going to have a security guard during the afternoons and at night. She said, "Maybe after this all has passed, the girls can come help me some."

"Okay," Luz said. Sophie and Jim had apologized to the Silva family, and assured them it was all completely unexpected. Sophie said she felt safe here, never suspecting any trouble would come here.

Granddad said, "Little girl, I don't mean to scare you. I've just got a gut feeling that more trouble is coming, and we want to do everything we can to protect you. We want you to stay here until after the wedding."

She said, "I don't want to be so much trouble."

He said, "Little girl, you have never, nor will you ever be trouble to us. You are, and always have been, a part of this family." Tears were pouring down all their faces. He said, "Promise me that you won't go back to that house without Jim or myself with you. Okay?"

"Okay," she said. She cried in his arms. She said, "I'm so sorry. I brought trouble and danger here. I never dreamed any of this would ever happen."

"Of course you didn't, because that's not the kind of person you are. Trust me and Jim, and don't let anyone lure you into going back there until Jim moves in with you." He said, "We are getting cameras and security alarms installed."

"Thank you, Granddad," she said, and hugged him. They were all exhausted from the stress and tears of the day. They prayed and all slept well.

> *The Lord is my strength and shield. I trust him with all my heart. He helps me. And my heart is filled with joy. I burst out in songs of Thanksgiving.*

> —Psalm 28:7

CHAPTER 16

Sophie had not yet secured a doctor. She called Russ Oliver's OB-GYN office. They had a cancelation on Monday with Russ. She explained her situation, and they secured her medical records from her OB. When Russ checked her over, he said she and Abby were doing great. She asked him who he used as a pediatrician with his twins, and he gave her a recommendation so she could get in right away. They made her an appointment for Thursday to do an ultrasound. Russ said, "I will need to see you every week until she makes her grand entrance."

"Okay," Sophie said. Jim asked her all about her appointment and how she and Abby Grace were doing.

He said, "I'd like to go with you to your appointment and see her ultrasound."

She said, "You have missed so much work because of me, you don't have to do that."

"I want to be there for you and Abby Grace, always."

She replied, "You are, and have been. You've risked your life for us."

He said, "That's what love does."

"You're the best," she said, and kissed him. As she and Jim were making plans on Wednesday, she said, "You will move in with me on our wedding night, right?"

"Yes," he said. She had a concerned look on her face. He took her hand and said, "Sophie, you can say anything to me. What are you thinking?"

She said, "I need time to adjust to having you living with me every day. I'm not comfortable sleeping in the same room yet." He snuggled her close and kissed her head.

Then he said, "Sophie, we have years to catch up. I have no problem with sleeping in separate rooms until you are ready for us to take the next step."

Sophie said, "Thank you for understanding."

Jim said, "I will get a woman officer to stay here with you during the day, or Gran, if I have to go out, but I plan to work from home, our home, and I will try to be easy to adjust to. I want to treat you and Abby Grace like the princesses you are."

She said, "Gregory was not very happy with me."

He said, "He didn't love you, or know you. Since he wasn't a prince, he didn't know how to treat a princess. Sophie, look at me. I know that our Father God put us together. Don't listen to the enemy of your soul; remember he is a liar." He leaned over and kissed her and said, "We are going to be fine." He kissed her tears away, and their lips met again. She felt everything would be all right. In a few minutes, he asked her if she thought Connie and Debbie would consider moving here. He said, "There's less opportunity here, and a smaller pay scale, but it's more laid-back, less smog and traffic."

"Amen," she said.

He said, "It would be easier for you here if your friends were here."

She said, "Yes, it would, but either way, I'm here to stay."

"Great," he said, "I'd hate to have to move to Atlanta."

She smiled and said, "I don't see that happening. I think they would love it here. They said they would check it out this weekend, but there won't be a lot of time, but we will make some.

"You said you'd keep it simple."

"I did," she said. "Connie has two years' experience as a teacher. She teaches kindergarten, like me. She's not been lucky with dating and is ready for a fresh start. Debbie will have her RN in the spring and hasn't met her special someone yet. She wants to work with the elderly. She helped care for her grandparents."

He said, "Well, there is a large assisted living near here. Maybe you girls could pop in for a look this weekend."

"Maybe so," she said. "We will see what all we can squeeze in. I would really love to have them here."

"So would we," Jim said. "Your friends are great." And in the back of his mind, Jim was thinking, *Which single Christian guys do I know that I could maybe set these girls up with? I'm gonna have to give that some serious thought.*

CHAPTER 17

Thursday morning, Sophie found her dress, and it was perfect. She didn't think she would be able to find one so beautiful. They assured her she would have it by Saturday. In case it didn't fit, she'd have time to get another. She told the girls to pick a simple summer dress in a solid summer color, and she would order it. They did and got next-day shipping. All their dresses fit. (They FaceTimed with Gran.) Sophie's was ivory, Connie's a soft coral, and Debbie's a soft blue. Gran chose a lovely soft pink. Sophie had an ivory pillbox hat, with a little lace that came down over the eyes and face. It had some ivory pearls on it that was her grandmother Brewer's. She had worn it when she and Sophie's grandfather had their fiftieth wedding anniversary celebration. It was in a hatbox in the top of Gran Brewer's closet. It looked new, and Sophie loved it. It suited her and matched the ivory of her dress well. Sophie couldn't find her grandmother's ivory pearl earrings; she figured Gregory had found them. She said, "I need to go get ivory pearl earrings."

Jim's gran said, "I would be honored if you would wear mine."

Sophie wiped tears and said, "I would be honored to. Now shoes, and I'm set." She and Gran went by Sophie's mailbox as they came back from shoe shopping. As they pulled up, Sophie opened the box, and among the mail was a handwritten note saying, "You will pay," scribbled roughly with a crayon.

Sophie and Gran said, "What is that?"

"Get out of here," Sophie said. "Head for the police station." As they were going, she called Jim and said, "I have a piece of disturbing mail. Gran and I are heading to the police station."

"It's not a package, is it?"

"No."

"I will meet you there," he said.

Gran said, "Oh, God, protect us," and she sped up.

"What is it?" Sophie said as they were hit from behind and knocked off the road. The angle was all that kept them from rolling over as they went down the embankment and landed in a branch. Gran grabbed her purse as she was asking Sophie if she was okay. Sophie was shocked when she saw the gun. Gran was unbuckled and looking around.

She said to Sophie, "Do you recognize that man coming?"

"No," Sophie said. She then said, "This wasn't an accident, was it?"

"No," Gran said. "It wasn't."

The man asked, "Is anyone hurt?"

Gran lowered the window and said, "We were just trying to figure that out. I think we are okay."

He said, "Would you like me to help you out of the vehicle?"

"Hold on." Her phone rang. It was Granddad.

"Where are you? Grace, are you two okay?"

"We think we are. We're off the road out by Stagg's Road, please come with backup. We were run off the road."

He said, "We're on our way. Stay on the line." He told Jim and Sgt. Talley what was going on. Then Sgt. Talley got on the radio and called for any and all vehicles in the area to respond and told them the appropriate codes. Granddad and Jim were overjoyed when they saw two faces smile at them. People tried to get them to get out of the SUV, but they insisted they were fine there until their husbands arrived. Gran laid her purse over the gun but kept her hand on it. It made Sophie feel safer. When their guys got there, she put it back in her purse. The police had everyone go back up to the roadside and give statements.

Gran looked to the officers and said, "We were run off the road by a new, or almost new, Silverado pickup, navy blue. He ran up on the back of me and hit me. I only saw one person. He looked to be tall, medium build."

"Could you recognize him?"

"No," she said. "He was wearing a cap."

"Sophie, did you see him?"

"No," she said, "I was looking at this."

Jim had just opened her door and said, "What?"

She handed him the note.

"Where did you get this?"

"This was what was in the mailbox."

"What were you doing at the house?"

"We were just checking the mail and I found the note and told Gran to get us to the police station. Someone was there and followed us. Then ran us off the road."

"Are you sure you are okay?"

"Yes, I feel fine."

Gran assured them she was fine. She said, "I asked God to protect us, and you can see He did."

Jim laid his hand on Sophie's abdomen and said, "We need to get you two checked out."

"No," she said, just as Abby kicked his hand good. "We are fine," she assured him. Granddad and Jim took them home. They needed some recliner time. The three policemen stopped the truck twenty minutes from town. They said they had to run him down and set up a roadblock. They ran the plates and called for backup. Apparently, the truck was stolen! The driver was Gregory's best friend, Rodney. The one who had broken into the lake house. Sure enough, the truck had been wrecked on the front bumper. They arrested him and booked him on two counts of attempted murder, reckless driving, driving a stolen vehicle, evading police, and hit-and-run.

Sgt. McKinny said, "He's not going anywhere. The judge will not allow him to post bail. Hopefully, his friends are not around. Keep your eyes open, and I will put extra patrol cars in the area. Stay safe and alert."

Sophie wanted to walk after dinner. They invited Gran and Granddad. Granddad said, "I will keep my eyes open here. We will walk when you two get back." While Sophie was in the bathroom, Granddad said "Jim, do not go out there without a gun."

Jim turned around, and Granddad saw the gun in his belt. "Stay safe out there, keep those eyes and ears open."

"Always, I've got to protect my princesses."

"Amen," Granddad said. "You two enjoy the walk."

"Will do," Jim said. His eyes were very diligent. After going into the sanctuary and praying, Sophie went to the restroom, and Jim walked out toward the lake so he could keep an eye on her and see a lot of area. As he looked down to the lake area behind Sophie's lake house, his eye caught something. There was a man on a small boat, taking pictures toward the back of the lake house. Jim wished he had a good camera with a zoom lens. He took a few pictures anyway. Sophie walked up, and he said, "Go wait for me in the chapel. Stay over to the side out of sight."

"What's he doing down there? What are you doing?" she asked with alarm in her voice.

He said, "He is taking pictures of the house. I want pictures of him. You stay in there safe. I'm going to get closer." He saw she was concerned, so he kissed her and said, "You pray for me to get a good picture and not get seen. Call and talk to someone at the police station and tell them I think the guy in the boat is waiting for the guy in the truck. Go, sweetheart." She did, and he eased around getting pictures. He gave a loud bird call. Kyle looked that way, and Jim got a good picture. The cops got in a boat around the lake and got some good pictures. He spotted them and took off. Jim had gotten really close and got pictures that could identify the boat. Policemen combed the area to see if anyone was hanging around. No one was sighted. Sophie heard Jim's bird call as he was getting close. She came out to see him and was so excited to see he was okay. He too was relieved. He had been praying for her safety.

As he navigated down the hill trying to get a close picture without being seen, he took her hand, and as they started walking back, she said, "I've got to go to the restroom again, sorry."

He chuckled and said, "You don't have to apologize. If I had all that weight on my bladder, I'd probably be saying 'me first.'"

She laughed and said, "And I'd say 'get behind a tree.'"

He leaned in and got a kiss and said, "I will be right here." She came out and didn't see him.

She called, "I'm here." He came toward her from the side with a beautiful bouquet of wildflowers.

He said, "I'm sorry. I thought I'd have enough time to get these. Forgive me for frightening you. That's the last thing I want to do." He took her hand, she looked into his face, and got lost in his gorgeous blue eyes. They went into each other's arms. He whispered into her hair, "You feel like the other half of me that's been missing since I was fifteen." She squeezed him so hard he could barely breathe. He kissed her, and they both felt it to their toenails. As he walked with her back to his grandparents', it was so peaceful, even with all that had transpired today. It seemed like their lives were being torn apart, and yet at the same time, they were coming together after all these years. And hopefully for a lifetime. Walking the well-beaten path, and their prayers were being answered. The weapons formed against them were not prospering. They felt like they could live here peacefully for years, leading Abby Grace along the well-beaten path. Teaching her to love the Lord and His sanctuary, and any other children He might bless them with. Each of their hearts was thinking about these things. He stopped and kissed her again, and as Abby was kicking him, he said, "I've got to be the luckiest man alive. I am so blessed."

"So am I," she said.

There was a police car in the drive. They went around to the front where they asked and answered some questions. Jim pulled up a close-up of the guy on the boat, showed it to Sophie, and knew immediately by the look on her face she knew him.

She said, "It's Gregory's brother Kyle. Oh my god. We are not safe here," as she broke down crying. They were all comforting her. Jim and Sophie went back to the police station, and she told them what was going on. They told them they are going to alert Marietta and Atlanta and put his pictures out there, with hopes they will have him in custody before morning. They placed a police car at their driveway, and they all prayed for the officers' safety as well as theirs.

CHAPTER 18

Friday was so exciting. The girls were coming! Yeah! Wedding plans face-to-face. The security alarms were on, cameras everywhere. Jim still didn't want Sophie and the girls to be there at the lake house. He insisted they stay at Gran and Granddad's. He said, "Those guys are out of jail on bond and know how to find you. Sophie, I can't lose you."

She said, "We are safe in Jesus. We are gonna be okay. I'm sorry I fell apart on you yesterday. I don't think they are coming back. We have security. You and Granddad put the fear of the Lord in them. They have gotten caught every time; and every weapon formed against us has failed. We will be okay. I'm sure they are not coming back."

Sgt. McKinney said, "Kyle has been arrested, and the judge is not going to grant him bail."

Sophie said to Jim, "You and I have a wedding in a week with lots to do in the meantime." They all went over all their lists, reminders, and decided what to do first thing tomorrow. Jim called the guard at the end of the driveway and said they were gonna walk later as they talked of God's presence and favor and blessing.

Granddad looked at Connie and Debbie and said, "Your blessings are coming. Father God has a plan for you two also. He sees your hearts, your love and concern, and your faithfulness." Tears rolled down all their cheeks. They all took turns sharing a verse that had spoken to them. They were all at peace. Granddad still gathered them all in a circle and prayed. "Yeah, we've got us a wedding next Saturday." Everyone agreed the wedding should be at the sanctuary.

It had been such a special place for them all. They called Kelly, and Ahna asked her to clean early Saturday morning. She said she could, and they invited the two of them to the wedding and reception. They went and looked at cakes. Gran knew a lady with a shop across her yard from her house. Her cakes were always fresh and delicious. Sophie chose a very simple white cake, small three, six, nine-inch layers. No color on it except for a simple silver cross on top, and three silver hearts touching the one in the middle, larger; it represented Jesus. They also ordered her Black Forest cake for the groom's cake. It was one of Jim's favorites. Then they ordered flowers to be delivered between eight and eight forty-five. The caterers were set up.

Gran said, "We have used them for years, for all kinds of holidays and celebrating. They kept everything very simple." It was a very productive day. They had a nice lunch in town. Russ was Jim's best man, and Jim invited several friends from work and church to the wedding. He had some friends he wanted Connie and Debbie to meet. He explained he and Sophie had been each other's first loves. She had to move away, but she came back here after the death of her husband, and also that she was expecting.

He said, "We've been seeing each other and have decided to go ahead and marry now because I worry about her when I leave her every evening." The Silva family, of course, was coming. They ended up with at least forty coming to attend. They sat on the porch Saturday night, listening to the rain, and thanking God for His blessings, while eating frozen yogurt. Jim said, "I pray it doesn't rain next Saturday."

Sophie said, "It won't. I've prayed, and I'm believing." It had been an amazing day. They were all tired as they circled in prayer and said good night. They got up and went to church Sunday morning and had lunch at Gran and Granddad's after. Then the girls headed home. Sophie and the Nelsons all took a good nap and relaxed to a good movie. Later they went for pizza before church in the evening, walked from the church to the ice cream parlor, and back to Granddad's truck. They talked about the goodness of God all the way home, prayed, and they all had a restful night's sleep.

CHAPTER 19

Monday morning after her Bible reading, as she was enjoying her tea with Gran, Sophie looked back over the weekend and all the things that had been accomplished. She said "Lord, I am one blessed woman. To have such a wonderful family and friends who are here for me. And to get the opportunity to get back the love of my life. And soon I will be holding a precious baby girl. Bone of my bone, flesh of my flesh." She placed her hand on her tummy and said, "Little girl, you are so loved and will be so spoiled!"

Gran said, "Amen. I made you something."

"When have you had time?" Sophie asked.

Gran said, "I worked on it while you and Jim were walking."

Sophie said, "You amaze me, Gran."

Gran said, "Come with me." She took Sophie to her bedroom and said, "Here are the pearl earrings."

"Thanks," Sophie said as Gran handed her a small gift bag and the box with the earrings. Sophie opened the bag and cried.

Gran said, "Something old, something new, something borrowed, and something blue. Now you have it all." Sophie marveled at Gran's handiwork: a blue handmade handkerchief with a small silver cross embroidered on the corner and three silver hearts touching with the center larger one representing Jesus. Sophie cried and hugged Gran.

"You are the best," she said.

Gran said, "I made Jim a matching one."

"Thank you, Gran. You are such a blessing."

Gran said, "I am honored to be a part of God's plan for your lives." She laid a hand gently on Sophie's tummy and said, "I can't wait to meet this little girl, and hold her, and be a part of her life."

"Amen," Sophie said. As Jim walked her to the sanctuary that night, she was having Braxton Hicks contractions but didn't tell him. She thought of the fact the girls would be staying at the house Saturday, with all their stuff, and it was her wedding day.

She brought it up, and Jim said, "It's okay. I will sleep in the den."

She said, "That just doesn't seem right."

He said, "It would not be in the standard situation, but we're not in that one." He smiled and said, "I would sleep on the porch just to be closer to you. Now no more worries. We are doing great," and he kissed her till she tingled. It made her think of an old song, "I Wanna Be Loved," and so she knew what she wanted to dance to after the wedding, and to her surprise, Gran had the album and a phonograph player and more old love songs. They made a playlist and played them to see how they flowed together. Karen agreed to be the DJ, and she practiced while Gran and Granddad practiced dancing. It was beautiful and precious. As they played the second song, "Have I Told You Lately That I Love You?" she saw a special look between Gran and Granddad, as he put out his hand. It was beautiful to experience the love that passed between them. They danced perfectly together. On the next song, Granddad held his hand out to Sophie, they danced, and she cried. Her dad, granddad, nor brother would be there. She knew Granddad was saying, "I'm here for you."

The next dance, he danced with Karen, then said, "Wonderful dancing, beautiful little lady, you go home before it gets dark. You've got this." She beamed a beautiful smile.

Sophie said, "You can bring a friend or two if you'd like, male or female."

"Really?" Karen said.

"Really," said Sophie.

Jim came in from showing a building. "Did you convince them to buy?"

"I did," he said. He reached a hand over to Sophie's tummy and said, "We have to stay number one in the real estate market and secure a future for our girl here. I've already started a savings account for her."

Granddad said, "I deposited $50,000 in her account." They both were overwhelmed and cried, and they thanked him. Granddad said, "We made at least that much on the deal you just closed. Well, I have an appointment to close on another one on Wednesday."

"Great!" they all said.

"Have you all been dancing?"

"Guilty," they all said.

"Well, let's practice," and they did. Then they had apple pie, did a Bible study, prayed, and slept peacefully, thankful for a blessed day.

CHAPTER 20

Tuesday flew by. Tuesday night, Sophie put on the song again and asked Jim to dance. They danced very well together, even with Abby Grace in the middle. Jim said, "I love this song!"

"Good." Sophie said. "Because it's the one I want to dance to on our wedding day, and the night we two become one."

He knew what she meant and said, "I like that being our song."

She said, "Do you have any songs you'd like to have played at the reception?"

"Yes. "Have I Told You Lately That I Love You?""

She said, "It's already number two on the playlist."

He said, "Then I trust you to finish the list," and as he kissed her. He said, "I don't know how it's possible, but I love you more with every passing day."

"I know what you mean," she said. "Each day, we grow with whatever it brings, and God is pouring out blessings daily. It's amazing how everything has come together. We never expected all the things that went wrong, but everyone is so supportive and helpful. No one has said 'I can't do what you need.' Only our Father in heaven could pour out such blessings."

"I agree," he said, and he held her hands between his, and offered up a prayer of Thanksgiving to Father God. After church Wednesday night, they walked downtown.

She said, "How can you want to parade this fat lady down the streets?"

He said, "I want everyone to see my chestnut-haired beauty and see I'm the happiest man in the world." She cried, and he stopped, dried her eyes, gave her a big kiss and said, "That will give them something to talk about." They went into the local ice cream parlor and enjoyed a shared banana split and cups of ice water. She pottied, and they walked back to the church and got the car.

As they drove back to Gran's, she said, "I know we walked downtown, but I'd still like to walk to the sanctuary."

"Then we shall," he said. As they walked back, he asked if he could come to her OB appointment.

She said yes.

Then Jim said, "I've got me a date." She bopped him on the shoulder. "Hey!" he said. "Don't beat up on a guy for being happy and blessed."

She beamed him a big smile as they walked back to the sanctuary. Sophie said, "Smell the flowers, isn't that a beautiful fragrance? It will be more so on our wedding day. We have some wonderful ones coming. I've ordered lots of colorful fragrant blossoms. I've prayed for that day many times through the years."

Jim said, "Me too."

She said, "And we both thought we lost each other, and God has given us a second chance."

"And an extra blessing," he said as he looked at her tummy.

CHAPTER 21

Thursday morning, Jim took her to her OB appointment. He saw several people he knew as Sophie signed in. Jim shook hands with each of them and introduced her as his fiancée. He made her feel loved and special, and she saw how respected he was in the community. As they were called back, he saw Russ down at the end of the hall about to go into a room. Russ gave him a thumbs-up. After they took her vitals, she was sent to get blood drawn and do a urine sample. They had Jim wait in the exam room. Sophie was back quick. Russ came in and told Jim it was good to see him, shook hands, and said hello to Sophie, asked lots of questions, checked her over, and said that little girl has a warrior's heartbeat, strong. He told Sophie, "You are measuring about thirty-seven weeks. I want to do one more ultrasound. She seems well positioned, but I want another picture."

"Okay," she said.

He said, "Brenda, our ultrasound technician will be here soon, and I will meet you in there soon." Abby Grace was beautiful and sucking her thumb. She had a good covering of hair.

Brenda said, "She is five pounds, eleven ounces now, and she will gain probably a pound, and maybe a little more before birth. She is a beauty."

Jim said, "Look at her mom. She is going to look just like her. I'm a blessed man."

"Amen," Russ said, and patted him on the back. He told Sophie, "Everything is great. See you two on Sat. Stop up front and make an appointment for next week. I will want to see you weekly. If you have any problems, call twenty-four hours a day. I have an answering service."

As they left, Jim said, "What sounds good for lunch?"

"Anything that doesn't bite back," she said. He got tickled and grabbed her and hugged her on the sidewalk. His face glowed with joy, and hers did too. They had a wonderful lunch. He took her back to Gran's to rest. After her nap, she told Gran about her appointment and Abby's progress, as promised.

Gran said, "I'm making meatloaf, biscuits, mashed potatoes, and fried green tomatoes for dinner."

"Oh, Gran, that sounds wonderful. Can I help?"

"You bet," Gran said. "What do you want for dessert?"

"A butter and jelly biscuit," Sophie said. "I can walk it off after dinner; that dress has to fit Saturday."

Gran smiled and said, "Oh, it will fit." Dinner was great. Sophie and Jim cleaned up the kitchen, and then they all walked back to the sanctuary. Kelly and Ahna were just leaving the sanctuary, so Sophie got to meet them. They loved each other immediately. They felt the spirit in each other. Kelly and Ahna were both so beautiful. Both had a heart for God. Ahna had given her heart to Jesus recently, and Gran had bought her a Bible when she found out. Kelly and Ahna were excited about the wedding. Sophie asked if they would like to be in the wedding.

Kelly said, "You don't even know us. Why would you ask us to be a part of your wedding?"

A few tears rolled down Sophie's cheek, and she said, "Because you have taken care of my very special place."

Tears rolled down Kelly's face, and she said, "You will never know what this place means to me. I need this little sanctuary." They held each other and cried. No one had a dry eye.

Sophie said "I knew it was special to you because you took such good care of it. I was overjoyed when I came back and saw it so clean. Thank you." So, before they left, they had all prayed together, and Sophie had talked them into meeting her in town the next day to get dresses. Then they would all have dinner together.

CHAPTER 22

Friday, Sophie woke up so excited and happy. "One more day, and I get to marry the man I have loved for years." She thanked Father God for another day. She did her Bible reading, a little cleaning and laundry, talked with Gran and Luz, and hosed down the porches. After a smoothie, put her feet up and napped. Before meeting Kelly and Ahna in town, they found Ahna a beautiful pink and purple dress—her favorite colors. Kelly chose a blue; it was a different shade than Debbie's. She also bought them new shoes, and they found a nice little basket for the flower girl, and had time to stop in the florist to get some drooping roses to make petals for the flower girl basket. The florist heard them talking about going to dinner. She had a small Styrofoam cooler and put the roses in there so they wouldn't turn brown from the heat. They also got pink and purple ribbons for the basket.

Kelly hugged her and said, "Thank you so much for including us in your special day."

Sophie said, "I hope you and Ahna will always be a part of our lives. I can't wait for you to meet my Abby Grace." She looked at Ahna and said, "Abby will need a friend, do you want to feel her move?" Ahna shyly nodded. Sophie took Ahna's hand and placed it on her tummy. Abby Grace gave a good kick.

Ahna giggled and asked, "When is she gonna get out?"

"Oh, two to three weeks." Then she looked at her watch and said, "We've got to go. See you two at the restaurant." They all had a wonderful time, a wonderful meal, and great fellowship. Connie and Debbie were glad to see Sophie had a lot of new friends. They all took a good walk around town after dinner and said their good nights. Jim was staying at the lake house with the girls that night, and the wedding was starting at eleven o'clock, so he left for Grans at eight thirty. The flowers were arriving by nine. Kelly was there cleaning when Luz arrived to meet the flower delivery. She and her girls were going to decorate. Luz's husband, Armando, was putting down three carpet runners and setting up a small water station with the little eight-ounce water bottles on ice. This wedding day was coming together well.

CHAPTER 23

The wedding day

When Luz and Kelly were finished, the little sanctuary was spotless, with an open Bible on the altar. It was opened to Psalm 23. Pastor Cliff was gonna read it in the ceremony. It was special to Sophie and Jim. After the reading, and before their covenant to one another before God, they were going to take communion. Luz had it all set up for them. There was a wonderful breeze coming off the lake, carrying the fragrance of the beautiful flowers through the air. Joy filled the air, music was playing, they were testing the volume. It was amazing how fast it all came together. They had everything they needed and more. When Sophie had gotten up, everyone was still asleep. She had walked out on the back screened porch, lifted her arms, and thanked her Father in heaven for His love, mercy, grace, every blessing of life, and for this day. It was beautiful—blue skies, sunshine, and a wonderful breeze. She had to force herself to eat. She was so excited. Today Cinderella marries her prince. Tears started all around the room. Jim had already left for Gran's. Sophie had insisted on walking up the beautiful well-beaten path to meet Jim. She had no idea that Luz and Kelly had decided to scatter flower petals all along the path. It was beautiful and fragrant. As was the entire area around the little sanctuary.

The wedding party at the top, in front of the sanctuary, began to assemble. They had three photographers. One three-fourths of the way up the path, one at the top focusing on the bridal party, then the bride and groom. They were determined to get both their faces as they saw each other for the first time on their wedding day. Or so they thought. He had kissed her this morning. As Sophie started up the path, she stopped, looked up, and said, "Thank you, Granddad. I believe you, Gran, and all of my family in heaven are watching. Thank you for building the beautiful little sanctuary that has blessed all our lives."

"Stop that crying," the girls said.

"They are happy tears," Sophie said. They all started up the path again. Jim was breathless when he saw her. She was so beautiful. That chestnut hair was stunning, blowing in the breeze all around her shoulders. He loved the hat; he had known nothing of it. He could see only her in her beautiful dress as she gracefully walked toward him, so handsome in his navy suit, blue shirt, and silver tie. Everyone was looking from one of them to the other; it was magnetic, as their eyes never left each other.

He said, "Wow, you look amazing."

"So do you, my prince."

He said, "I love your dress, and I love that hat on you."

"Then I shall wear it every year on our anniversary."

"I'd love that," he said. It was as if they were alone. They couldn't take their eyes off each other. Everyone was watching with fascination. No one interrupted. Then he took her hand and kissed it and said, "Shall we?"

"Yes," she said, looking at him with wonder in her eyes. Into the chapel they went. Only Pastor Cliff was inside. He welcomed everyone and thanked them for coming to witness the joining of the two of them as they make their covenant with God into holy matrimony. Pastor Cliff read the twenty-third Psalm. They took communion. Then said their vows. It was a beautiful, simple wedding. They had told the pastor their stories, and he was glad to be a part of this blessed wedding day. The photographers took a lot of pictures, being careful to block her tummy in some of the pictures. They had made a special wooden sign for the sanctuary, telling who built it and what year, and that it was for family, community, and friends. They stood behind it. It was a perfect photo to display. It hid her tummy. It was Gran's idea. She knew Sophie would want Abby Grace to be old enough to understand before she saw some of the pictures. There was a beautiful rose bush in full bloom. They took a picture behind it. And in the wedding party pictures, they stood Ahna in front of her. It worked perfectly. And they got a great picture of them leaving the wedding. Sophie had no idea, but Jim had arranged a horse-drawn, Cinderella-type carriage.

She said, "I heard a horse," as they were about finished with the photos, and as she turned, she saw it; she wept. They got them standing in front of the carriage, with her bouquet in front. It totally hid her tummy, then she and Jim were in the carriage. They also put the bouquet in front of the baby. Jim needed another kiss, and it was a good one.

"Wow, Mrs. Nelson, that was an amazing kiss."

"I'm glad you liked it, because I plan to give you several of those every day for the rest of my life."

"I sure hope so," he said.

She said, "I hear you, Mr. Nelson." They held hands and enjoyed the short ride to Gran's. The photographers were the best; they missed nothing.

CHAPTER 24

The reception

One of the photographers had gone ahead and was filming their arrival in the carriage, and Jim helped her out. You would have to look closely to tell she was almost eight and a half months pregnant. Everyone clapped and cheered as they walked from the carriage. The day was perfect. God had blessed them beyond their wildest dreams. As they approached the back deck at Gran's, it was decorated so beautifully. Sophie had no idea the work that was being done. Ivory lace tablecloths, and so many flowers that the fragrance in the air was heavenly. Sophie was so in awe of what her Heavenly Father had done, and so quickly. Granddad and Gran spoke and thanked God for bringing Jim and Sophie back together, and for Abigail Grace, who would join them soon.

Granddad prayed, thanking God for a beautiful day filled with hope, promise, joy, family and friends, and prayed blessing over the food. He said, "As soon as these two dance to the song they have chosen, we shall all eat, dance, and be merry." Jim and Sophie danced to the old song "I Wanna Be Loved." Then everyone danced to "Have I Told You Lately That I Love You?" Then they ate, enjoyed the cake cutting and the cake. Danced some more, fellowshipped, and about two thirty, it began to cloud up. Everyone began to go. The caterers fixed plates of food and cake for Jim, Sophie, and the girls as they prepared to go.

Jim leaned down to Sophie and said, "Mrs. Nelson, are you ready to go home?"

"Yes," she said, "I'm really late for my nap."

They all laughed, and Gran said, "Get home to that recliner, missy."

She grinned at Gran and said, "I'm gettin'." They all laughed.

Jim kissed his grandparents' cheeks and gave them big hugs and whispered, "You two need a recliner break also."

"We hear you," they said, and picked up their plates of food and cake and went inside. Back at their lake house, they all got in comfy clothes and took a nap. After their naps, Sophie got up. They were all in the kitchen. She heard Jim trying to convince them again that they should move here.

She said, "Did you all leave me some cake?"

"We did." And Jim told the girls of opportunities in the area. He said, "We do have a singles Bible study at church, with a few worthy candidates. Did any of the single guys at the wedding and reception catch your eyes?"

"Interestingly," Debbie said, "I talked to Chris, and we had some things in common. I thought he was gonna ask me out for a second there, but someone called him away."

"What about you, Connie? I saw you talking with Jordan."

"Yes," she said, smiling. "I liked him."

"Well," Jim said, "maybe we could invite them to dinner Saturday night."

Debbie said, "We can't come next week, but maybe the week after." They ate again and walked out back by the lake. Then they came in and played Chicken Foot Dominoes.

Sophie said, "I wonder how many people spend their wedding night playing games with friends."

"I don't know," Debbie said, "but I'm having a good time." They all laughed and agreed. Before they all went to bed, they all joined hands and prayed and thanked Father God for His blessings and asked for a good night's rest.

Jim kissed Sophie good night and said, "See you in the morning, beautiful."

A big "AMEN," she said. "Yahoo! I finally got my man."

He kissed her till she tingled, and said, "Till tomorrow."

CHAPTER 25

Sunday morning

Everyone was up by seven thirty and showered by eight. Sophie was a tea drinker, and so were the girls, but she knew Jim was a coffee drinker in the morning. So she had asked Gran the week before the wedding to show her how much coffee to add to make two cups. And she had practiced. She knew he liked it just coffee, nothing added, and that he would eat any muffins, although apple was his favorite. She and Gran had made several varieties that week and put them in the freezer. So this morning, there was a big platter of mixed muffins and a bowl of mixed berries and one of cut-up cantaloupe, which they all liked. She knew they were all having lunch in town before the girls headed back to Atlanta. So a light breakfast would be fine. Jim was the first one in the kitchen. He smelled the coffee, walked in, and said, "Wow, I like seeing you in the morning," and gave her a hug and kiss. He said, "Um, you smell good."

She said, "Right back at you. I love that fragrance you wear."

He said, "Gran bought it for me years ago, and I've stayed with it."

"Good decision," she said and snuggled up to him. Abby was kicking him.

He said, "Abby's jealous."

The girls walked in and Connie said, "Should we come back later?"

"Ha ha," Sophie said. "It's our first morning living together, and it's a beautiful one. The past week and a half don't count. Now we are Mr. and Mrs."

"Amen," Debbie said right behind her. "Yeah, breakfast is ready."

"Yes, let's eat!" As they sat down, Jim reached for hands and prayed. They ate, cleaned up, and headed for church. They enjoyed Sunday school and the church service. Everyone was so welcoming. Lunch after was amazing. Then the girls and Sophie cried as they left to go back home. They prayed for everyone's safety. The girls were still not back at their own apartments yet because of what happened at the lake, and how quickly it had all happened before they left.

As they were sitting after dessert, finishing tea and coffee, Granddad said, "Connie and Debbie, I know you were settled where you were living, and probably want to get back there. Yet I'm concerned about that happening. Sophie feels you might consider moving here."

"Yes," they both said.

Debbie said, "I don't have my degree yet, it will be late spring."

"What are the chances you can stay where you are till spring?"

"Good," she said.

"Do you feel safe?"

"Yes," she said.

Jim said, "Yes, and it could be possible that your car is wearing out, and you're driving farther. Well, when you come back next week, we will take care of that. You both think about what kind of car you want. We will go new car shopping!"

"I can't consider that till I graduate."

"Well, I'm going to get you both a new car," Sophie said. "Because you're both the best friends ever."

They both said, "We can't let you do that."

All the Nelsons said at once, "Of course you can."

"No, that's too much."

"It's very little considering all that you two have done for me. You've risked your lives for me. It's a done deal, no more argument."

Tears were rolling off their faces, then Granddad said, "We are not giving Sophie all the joy. When you come back next week, you need to look at house plans. Gran and I are gonna build you two a new house."

They both said, "We can't let you do that."

"It's gonna be done. You two are part of the family now."

"That's too much."

"God says it's not. So it's gonna happen."

Everyone was in tears. As they returned home, Jim said, "Wow, Mrs. Nelson, we are alone at last in our new home, and it's starting to rain. Since we might not get to walk outside today, I might have to chase you around the house." And he took a stance and put out his hands like he was gonna block her.

She said, "Hey, that's not fair. I have three disadvantages here."

"Three?" he said.

"Yes. I'm big with child, I'm stuffed with lunch, and it's my nap time."

"Well, you win this time, little lady. But I shall have my victory chase one day."

"Yes, you will, Mr. Nelson. And if you're lucky, I will slow down enough so you can catch me."

He chuckled and said, "I look forward to that day."

"Me too," she said and kissed him till he tingled. He nuzzled her neck, tickling her. She said, "You'd better stop, I'm about to wet my pants." She hurried toward the bathroom, and as she came out, they heard a sound, and a ball of fire was shot toward the back of the house.

Sophie screamed. Jim grabbed her and said, "Get in your car and head to Gran's." He grabbed her purse and his pistol and followed her out. He drove his truck from the garage and away from the house as another fire bomb hit. Two had missed. Jim called 911 and said, "I need a fire truck and police." Someone just firebombed my house. We will need more than one truck, these guys are serious," he said. As she called Granddad, Sophie was hysterical. She was crying hard as she stopped up on the side of the road, with sirens blazing headed that way. All of it had just woken up Jim's grandparents as their phone rang. Sophie was crying so hard they could barely understand her.

She said, "They are burning our house down."

"We are on the way." The security guard was there with Jim, trying to keep the flames down. By the time the fire department got there, the screened porch was gone, and the house was sustaining some damage. They got it out finally, and enough police and state troopers responded. They got all the guys. There were three of them. More of Gregory's friends. Sophie was walking back toward the house, still hysterical, and Gran was trying to stop her.

Sophie said, "Jim is in there."

Gran said, "They will get him out. Sophie, there's a lot of help down there, and we are all going to be okay."

Sophie said, "I can't lose him."

"You won't," Gran said. "Now for Abigail Grace, you need to calm down. Trust in the Lord with all your heart and lean not on your own understanding. In all your ways acknowledge Him and he shall direct your path."

"Thank you, Gran, I needed that," she said, and she saw them bringing Jim out on a stretcher and were headed toward the ambulance. He was on oxygen. Then Granddad came out, being assisted by a first responder. They both started running.

Granddad held up his hands and said, "We're okay."

Sophie was by Jim's side quickly. He opened his red eyes and said, "I'm okay. Just need a breath of air."

"Okay, don't talk, babe. Rest your voice. I'm here," she said.

They told Sophie they needed to take him in to be checked out and treated and probably they will keep him overnight. Gran was on Jim's side, with Granddad on her other. Gran was holding a hand in each direction. When the firefighters were done, the house was still livable. Most of the damage was the back porch, mudroom, storage room, and screened porch.

Jim was alive. He said, "Sophie, we are gonna be okay. We've just got to repair the porch."

She said, "You are hurt. Rest. I'm here, everyone is okay."

He said, "Granddad, I hear another ambulance coming."

He said, "It's for Tommy. He is in the same condition as you. They're patching him up now."

"We owe him," he said.

"Yes," she said, "we do. No more talking right now. Rest, we will talk after a while."

"Are you sure you're okay?"

"Yes, shhh."

"I know this was terrifying," the attendant said.

"Yes, it was," Sophie said, "and I just want to see everyone well and okay."

"A few days, and they will be fine," the attendant said. "Are you two ladies okay?"

"Yes," they both said. Gran went and pulled the car down to get Sophie and Granddad. Granddad got in and rested, while Sophie and Gran went in and got the things Sophie felt they would need for a few days. The fire chief went in with them. He had known the Nelsons all of his life, and Sophie's grandparents. They all headed to the hospital after checking on Tommy. They followed the ambulances. Gran and Granddad held hands on the way. Sophie was quiet as a church mouse. They knew she too was praying. Tommy and Jim were both kept overnight in the hospital. Jim told Sophie to go with Gran and Granddad.

"You and Abby need rest, so do Tommy and I. We will be good as new in a day or two. Go, sweetheart. See you tomorrow."

"Okay, love." He closed his eyes and fell asleep as they covered him in prayers. It was devastating, the memories were painful. Some contractors who had worked a lot of real estate jobs for Granddad and Jim brought out two crews a day. They had their house repairs done and the big screened porch all finished in a week so Abby Grace could come home to her lake house. They knew she would love growing up here like they had, and they were determined to live here in God's blessing like their grandparents had. As Sophie got back to Gran's, she called Connie then Debbie and begged them to be careful. She felt they could still be in danger. They assured her they would be watchful.

CHAPTER 26

Sophie and Jim talked someone into giving them a crash course in Lamaze. They had to call and cancel the first two days. Jim wasn't up to it. After the fire, the first class was hard on Jim. He had taken Lamaze classes with Jenna, and Sophie saw he was having memories and said, "We don't have to do this."

"We do," he said and gave her a smile. "I'm okay. We're gonna do this. Abby Grace is coming, ready or not."

She smiled and said, "I would prefer to be ready." They did three nights, and was supposed to do it next week. They told Sophie that she was a natural, which was good. On Saturday, one week from the wedding, Sophie was chatting with the girls who were going to have to wait till Sunday morning to come. Jim was mowing and weed eating. He had done Gran and Granddad's earlier, drank another water, and took a Gatorade to start again.

Sophie said, "I need to get off here and start lunch."

"Okay," the girls said. They were on three-way calling. Sophie was busying around fixing lunch and realized the cramps were coming regularly. She called the girls back and said, "Abby's getting ready to make an entrance, pains are consistent."

"Oh my gosh," they both said. "We are gonna grab a bag and head that way." Debbie's class was over.

They prayed for her and Abby and said, "See you soon." Sophie showered, and dressed, and as she came through, Jim was coming in from the mudroom shower, with a towel wrapped around the waist.

Sophie whistled and said, "Looking good."

He felt himself blush, and said, "Thank you, Mrs. Nelson."

"You're welcome," she said. "Your lunch is on the table."

"Are you not eating too?" Then he watched as she had a contraction, and said, "How far apart?"

She said, "Eleven minutes. Go eat while I get the little things together. Go. You are gonna need the strength."

He kissed her and said, "I need to dress, we have time to eat."

"I'm gonna put my hair up."

He said, "We're having a baby."

Jim finished lunch and called his grandparents and said, "Abby's about to make her appearance, we are leaving for the hospital."

"We're praying for a safe, easy delivery," Gran said.

"Okay, see you in a while."

Sophie had called Russ. He said to head for the hospital in the next few minutes. "Okay," she said.

He told her, "I will see you there soon." Abby moved fast. Sophie's pains were three minutes apart when they checked her, and she was dilated to six.

The nurse called Russ and said, "This baby isn't waiting around."

"I will be there in minutes," and he was. She was dilated to eight. He told her and Jim, "Everything is going great. It won't be long now." When Sophie started pushing, Abby was ready and was born quickly. Her first cry was so precious. Sophie looked up and thanked her Father in heaven. Jim cut the cord. They held up a seven-pound beauty, wrapped her, cleaned her face, and let Sophie see her a minute and hold her.

Then said, "We are gonna get her and you cleaned up."

Jim and Russ looked at an exhausted Sophie and said, "You did great. You are a natural."

Russ said, "You should do this at least a dozen times."

"As long as it's one at a time," she said. They all laughed.

Jim kissed her and said, "See you in a few minutes," and he went and spread the good news. Connie and Debbie had just gotten there.

"She is beautiful," Jim said. He was all smiles. There were hugs and congratulations all around, and he said, "Has anyone called Luz?"

"Doing it now," Gran said. In a few minutes, the nurse came and asked them all to wash hands before going to the room. They did, and after lots of love to Sophie and congratulations to both, they all had to see and hold Abby a second. Phone cameras going off like crazy. Sophie had fed her a few minutes before everyone came to the room. In about thirty-five minutes, Gran said, "Why don't we go eat and let mommy rest a bit?" So they did, and she and Jim told them what to bring them back. Abby started crying. Jim talked to her, and she stopped and was looking at him.

He said, "Hello again, beautiful. It's me, your daddy. I'm so proud of you, little girl. We are gonna have a great life together. You look like your mommy, and that's awesome, by the way."

She started getting fussy, and he said, "Do you need a dry diaper?" And she did, so he looked over at Sophie and said, "Little girls are easier than boys. They don't pee on you."

"True," she said. He picked her up, and she started crying.

He said, "Where are her bottles?"

She said, "She doesn't have any."

He said, "Why?"

She reached for her and started to open a section of her gown.

"Oh," he said, and watched in fascination as she shyly nursed Abby in front of him. She blushed.

"I've never seen anyone nurse a baby before."

She smiled, and after a few minutes, she took the breast away. Abby wailed. She put her to the other breast, and Abby nursed hungrily. Jim was overjoyed when she asked if he wanted to burp her.

"Sure," he said. She could see on his face it brought back memories. He breathed in the newborn smell of her, kissed her little cheek, and rubbed her back.

The nurse came in and said, "Are you spoiling that baby?"

"You bet," he said.

She said, "You will regret it when she wants you to do it 24-7."

"Um, you might be right," he said and put her down.

The nurse said, "Your vitals are perfect. Do you want to get up a minute?"

"Yes," she said. "I need to go to the bathroom." She did fine. As she was getting in the bed, a knocking on the door brought the girls,

Gran, and Granddad, and food. They were hungry. Everyone else cooed and carried on over Abby Grace as they ate.

Everyone left early, saying, "Call us if you need anything. Rest as often as you can." Sophie, Abby, and Jim had a good night. Abby ate about every two and a half hours. Jim helped every time. He took pictures of them sleeping, and thanked God for his blessings and cried for his son in heaven. He knew he would see him again and thanked God for that promise. He prayed for them and that God would help him be the best husband and father ever. They were so beautiful, sleeping so peacefully. He thought of all Father God had brought them through. One battle after another, and though it had gotten scary, he had brought them through. He felt great gratitude and thanked Him. At three in the morning, Sophie woke up hungry. He asked her what she would like to eat.

He said, "I'm hungry too." When he got back, Abby was nursing again. It was a beautiful sight. Sophie's hair was a mess, which he thought was gorgeous. Abby's hair was dark. He hoped it would be chestnut like her mom's, and he hoped her eyes turned emerald. He never asked about Abby's dad and didn't feel he should. Abby would always be beautiful. No matter the color of her eyes and hair. Abby didn't want to stop nursing.

Sophie said, "Enough, little girl." Jim took her and started burping her. Sophie said, "I can burp her while you eat."

"No way, you worked hard today and still have to make milk."

She said, "I wasn't the one mowing and weed eating for hours."

"No," he said, "you worked harder."

She said, "I am one blessed woman."

He said, "I got the best end of the deal; two for one." She smiled that smile that always made his heart do a flip-flop. As she ate and watched him burping and changing Abby, she loved it. He was such a gentle warrior, and she was praying that she was enough for him and prayed they would always love and respect each other like they did now.

CHAPTER 27

The girls came after breakfast. Jim had eaten something in the cafeteria. They had brought Sophie a good breakfast. They stayed with her while Jim went home and showered and shaved and felt much better. He was tired and knew Sophie had to be more so. She was such a trooper, so different in every way from Jenna. He believed Jenna had given her heart to Jesus as a child, but she never pursued a relationship with Jesus, like many people. They want the fire insurance, but not the lifestyle that helps them to actually have a relationship with Jesus. They have no idea what they are missing—the peace, the joy, the security when you know that you know the Lord Jesus has your back and you are held in Him. Only our stubborn will and unbelief can separate us from the love and acceptance of a loving Father who stands with open arms, more than willing to forgive us our sins and heal us from the damage done to us from those sins. As he was driving back to the hospital, he prayed for everyone he could think of. Then for all the world and the needs of the people. He was glad to see his girls. Sophie had showered and washed her hair and was nursing Abby Grace again. He burped her, and he told Connie and Debbie, "This is how it's done."

They said, "You're the pro." Gran and Granddad brought lunch for everyone, and about two o'clock, the girls headed back to Atlanta. They both had school the next day and knew Sophie and Abby were in good hands and every need would be met. Abby was fussy.

Gran said, "She is adjusting to a new environment, and she is sore from birth and being held so much. It's traumatic on their little bodies, they have left their safe place." Sophie and Jim were drinking up her wisdom. Jim began to remember from when James Micah was born. He was so happy to have Abby fill his empty arms. Gran got a clean washcloth and washed Abby's face and hair. She loved it. Gran spoke softly to her and said, "Tomorrow we will give you a warm bath." Abby was just watching and listening. Gran said, "You will love a warm bath. We just have to keep your belly button dry. We can, and your little body will rest and feel good." Her little eyes were closing.

Sophie said, "She knows and loves your voice, like I do."

Gran put Abby down and said, "What can I do for you, little girl?"

Sophie picked up Gran's hand and kissed it and said, "Just keep on loving me and helping me to grow."

Gran kissed her hand and said, "Close those tired eyes, both of you, and nap while she is." Her other hand had been scratching Jim's back, he was almost out. She pointed him to the recliner and whispered to Sophie, "Call if you need anything, and he loves to have his back scratched."

"I will remember," Sophie said. They both slept good till the nurse came in for vitals. Abby slept through it, so Jim fell back asleep. Sophie did too. She awoke in an hour to Jim walking the floor and quietly singing to Abby. It was beautiful. He was in his own world with her and didn't realize Sophie was awake and watching. She got two pictures before he even realized it. They were great.

CHAPTER 28

Monday morning, around nine thirty, Russ Came in and said, "Is the Nelson family ready to go home?"

"Yes," they said.

"Well, I saw Abby's pediatrician making his way through, so I think he will release her to go home. You two are doing great. I will get your release ready, and if you need anything, call. Otherwise, I will see you in six weeks." They were home in an hour. Gran came at eleven thirty, with lunch, and they gave Abby a warm bath after Sophie fed her.

Gran said she should take a long nap. "You two do the same," and they did. She slept three and a half hours. Jim brought a bell in case she needed him, and he slept three hours. They had lots of people call in the afternoon. Luz and the girls came and brought dinner. They each had to hold Abby Grace. Gran told them not to let Abby get used to a light. "When you are ready to put her to bed at night, don't worry, you will hear her. Put her to bed and turn out the light. Use a small flashlight to get up, or turn on the lamp, but keep it as dark as possible so she doesn't get her days and nights mixed up." She said, "You can even turn on the closet light when you nurse her at night, just barely open it." Sophie listened, and Abby slept five hours, nursed, and slept four more. So they had a good first night home. Jim had a monitor in his room and got up, and Sophie shooed him back to bed and thanked God for a good husband and that Abby's first night home was a good one.

CHAPTER 29

Jim stayed home all week. They had a great time with Abby Grace. They took a grand amount of pictures and videos. They walked in their backyard every evening, careful to shade Abby. Fall was in the air, but it was still quite warm in the afternoons. She loved the out-doors, especially the bird sounds. Debbie had called and said, "I'd really love to be with you all this weekend, but I have a major test next week, and I must study, but Connie's coming and has promised me videos."

"You bet," Sophie said. "We will miss you. When you get your degree remember, you are to move here with us."

"I will," Debbie said. The weekend flew by quickly. They had a good week. Abby was sleeping good and growing like crazy. Abby had her two-week checkup on Thursday. Jim was still working from home. He scheduled the afternoon off and went along. They all napped after. Jim brought Sophie a snack and drink while she was nursing Abby.

Then she said, "I can't take it anymore. I need to go to the sanctuary."

"Okay," he said, "I will put the water in the car."

She said, "I want to walk."

"Are you sure you're up to it?"

"Most definitely."

"Well then, Mrs. Nelson, I shall get the front pack carrier, you get a diaper bag and water."

"Yes, sir, Mr. Nelson."

As she started to walk away, he gently pulled her back and kissed her, and he said, "I am one blessed man."

She smiled and said, "I'm the blessed one. Oh, how I love you," and snuggled in his arms.

He whispered into her ear, "I love you more than I ever thought it was possible to love someone."

"Same here," she said. They were created to be together. The walk up the path was wonderful. She had so missed it, and as always, her heart would make a leap at the sight of the little sanctuary. Jim looked at her face light up like a child's at Christmas. As they were about to go in, she touched his arm, and he stopped and he felt what she was about to say. "Yes, let's dedicate her here now." She smiled and looked up and said, "Thank you, Father." They held each other's hands and prayed with Abby in the middle. Then they each put a hand on her little head and prayed the prayer of dedication for her.

As they left the sanctuary, he said, "I still want her dedication in the church next week."

"Me too," she said and squeezed his hand. Abby loved her outing. Sophie wrote it all in her baby book about Abby's first trip to the sanctuary and her first dedication. She absolutely loved motherhood, but she knew she wanted to space out their children, so she called in for a birth control prescription.

CHAPTER 30

Abigail Grace loved her first visit to church. Her dedication ceremony was beautiful and very special, and she was on her best behavior. They had hired the photographers from their wedding to get pictures and a video. Connie and Debbie were there, everyone from the wedding, and even Sophie's aunt Linda was there. Her daughter had given birth the day before Sophie's wedding. It was so good to see her and catch up. She spent a few days with them before heading back to Birmingham. Later in the week, as Sophie and Jim finished their Bible study one morning, Jim took her hand, and they prayed, and he said to Sophie, "This little girl is so precious. I'd like to have more children. But we need to space out our blessings, for our sakes and theirs."

She turned to face him and smiled, caught his face in her hands, and said, "I love you so much, my husband and strong warrior, I'm in total agreement. I have birth control pills."

He smiled and said, "You're the best. God has blessed us so much. We know that we're God-given soulmates. No doubts. We also know there will be times of butting heads. But our hearts and relationships with God will sustain us through the hard times life will bring." As they watched Granddad and Gran holding hands and walking together, they felt they would live together for many years, blessed by God the Father, Son, and Holy Spirit. Life was good. Abby was doing great. Both girls had their new cars and were picking colors for their new homes, still in awe of God's blessings. The girls were coming every other week, and life was going good. Connie had put in an application for a job at the school. They told her there were two teachers retiring next year and they would hold onto her application. Debbie was excited about moving, and they each had found someone to date here in Mountain Lake. They met the guys at the wedding, then they built their relationships at the singles Bible study at church. Connie was dating a wonderful guy named Jordan, who worked with computers and had his own store. Debbie was dating a photographer named Chris, who was a really great guy and a lot of fun. He kept them all laughing. Especially on game nights.

Sophie had tried her grandmother Stewart's homemade bread. She had been missing it. They all loved it and said it needed to show up for every game night and would be welcome at any occasion. On a rainy night, when Abby was almost six weeks old, Jim had been in the garage building shelves, came in and showered, and was eating a snack in the kitchen. He looked up, and Sophie was slowly walking toward him, wearing his shirt he gave her in the rain the day she moved to Atlanta. She was breathtaking in that shirt with her hair down. He could smell her wonderful vanilla lotion. She put out her hand. He could hardly breathe. When she led him down the hall, he heard their wedding song, I Wanna Be Loved. He thanked his Lord for bringing her back to him. They both did as they danced to their song, and he spent his first night in their room.

CHAPTER 31

Life was going good. Abby was two months old. Sophie was writing in her children's book. The girls were excited to be moving to Mountain Lake soon. Sophie was overjoyed about everything but the upcoming trials. Jim watched things carefully, especially Sophie and Abby. Security was around, and the cameras stayed on, along with the alarm system. They felt safe and happy. They both loved fall in Mountain Lake. They decided to have an early Thanksgiving with the girls and their boyfriends so they could all be with their individual families on Thanksgiving. Sophie said, "I love dressing. I can eat it several days in a row." She made a lot and put an extra pan in the freezer. Gran and Granddad didn't join. They were going out with some old friends who were in town. Sophie and the girls cooked all day, they had lots of food, and they all had a wonderful evening, and ended playing Chicken Foot Dominoes. Abby was a very good girl and loved the company. The girls stayed overnight, and they went shopping the next day. Jim offered to watch Abby. Sophie said, "It won't be a quick trip."

"I can handle her," he said. "Pump her a bottle and feed her before you go. We will be fine, I promise. You girls need some girl time."

Sophie gave him a big hug and said, "You're the best." The girls shopped for hours. Sophie checked on Abby twice, and they were fine both times, so they stayed out another hour and went home. Abby got so excited when she saw her mommy. She cooed and smiled and was soon hungry. She ate and napped as the girls heated leftovers. They all ate, and the guys were coming later with pizza. They watched a couple of movies, and as the girls chatted about Christmas, Jim was thinking what on earth he was going to get his girls for Christmas. He caught them aside when Sophie went to the restroom and said, "Help! I need ideas." They brainstormed and came up with some good ideas. They all had so much fun. Chris and Jordan also had fun. Little Abby was all over them, laughing and charming everyone. By movie time, she was worn out and ready for bed. They all ate too much and had a memorable evening. The girls decided they should make it a tradition. Early Thanksgiving with a day of shopping and movie night.

CHAPTER 32

They had a wonderful Thanksgiving with Gran and Granddad. The day after Thanksgiving, Sophie was ready for a tree. Jim and Sophie had the most wonderful time choosing a tree, picking out ornaments and decorations. Gran and Granddad babysat Abigail Grace. The three of them had the most wonderful time. Abby was cooing and loving all of the attention. She took a bottle from Gran when she got hungry. They all three enjoyed their evening together. Sophie and Jim had a wonderful time; they even did some Christmas shopping. They left at two thirty and got home at seven twenty. After all the stuff was carried in, Sophie nursed Abby and put her to bed while the guys put the tree in the stand and watered it. Gran scooped them some frozen yogurt. After a little table time, the two grans said good night and headed home.

Sophie said, "Do we want to decorate tonight or tomorrow?"

"I have no plans for tomorrow," he said.

"Sounds like tomorrow it is. Shall we do our Bible study and turn in early?"

"I like that plan." He smiled. By nine thirty the next morning, they were working on the tree, having a wonderful time. They sat Abby in the car seat where she could watch. She loved it. They had everything decorated in two hours. Sophie nursed Abby while Jim made them a ham sandwich and a piece of pie for lunch. Abby napped, they did their Bible study, and started wrapping gifts. It was a beautiful array of colors under a beautiful tree. They were taking inventory of what they had and still needed to get. When Abby woke up, as she looked at the tree, she squealed with delight. Jim said, "If she was a little older, we'd be in trouble. She would be unwrapping everything."

"Yes, next year will be much different," said Sophie. Saturday, they decorated a little outside, and Jim helped Granddad do some decorating at home. Then they all headed to the office complex and decorated inside and out. Gran had someone come on the Tuesday before and paint Christmas scenes on the windows, and they looked great. When they were finished, they were quite pleased. The company Christmas dinner was next Friday. They gave a generous bonus to each family, plus a large fruit basket. Everyone laughed, played games, pictures were made, and everyone had a grand time. The Christmas season brought lots of joy, beautiful sights, and sounds. Abby was growing and had everyone wrapped around her little finger. She loved the colors and lights. It was an amazing Christmas. They even got snow on Christmas Eve. Only two inches, but it was beautiful. They celebrated with the girls the week before. Connie got an engagement ring for Christmas. Debbie got a friendship bracelet. Sophie got a new coat, and boots for walking to the sanctuary. Jim got a new scarf, gloves, and winter boots. Sophie noticed his boots needed replacing. they all were blessed beyond measure with a healthy, happy Christmas and New Year.

The girls had a wonderful time on New Year's weekend thinking of Connie and Jordan's upcoming wedding, planning a summer wedding. Thinking of a place for a dream wedding, dresses, wedding colors. They each had a notebook, and they got a planning board and brainstormed. It was so much fun, especially when Connie tried to pick a wedding gown. It was harder than she had imagined. She chose a beautiful aqua color and soft rose as her wedding colors. Chris was fine with the colors, and as they started talking about where they were going to marry, Connie said, "It has to be somewhere that we are all safe."

Chris said, "I have an idea. There is a new inn being built there, so maybe we could rent the whole place for a week and have all our families there."

Connie said, "We can't afford that."

"I have a little nest egg," he said. "We can."

The more they talked, the more excited they all became. It was an hour's drive away, so the next Saturday, they all drove over and checked it out and fell in love with it. They were not going to put an announcement anywhere. They just made a tight-knit guest list and kept it simple. Everything was planned before the end of January. Then came Valentine's Day. They all had a steak dinner in town. Gran and Granddad joined them. It was a beautiful dinner. Then Chris got on one knee in front of Debbie, and tears spilled all around the table. Kelly and her date were across the room. She saw what was about to happen and got a good picture. What a night.

CHAPTER 33

Life was going so good. Gregory's friends had been tried in court for the break-in, and all of them got a sentence of ten years because of prior offenses. Then Kyle was tried for attempted murder and got fifteen years. In two weeks, the three who tried to burn the house down would go to trial. Sophie and Jim were hoping they would take a plea bargain instead of going to trial. Abby was five months old, and Sophie and Gran went to lunch the day after Kyle's sentencing. As they left the restaurant, a bird flew at Sophie's head. She ducked and covered Abby's head. A shot rang out, and blood went everywhere. Sophie and Gran went down. Sophie was on her side. Gran got a good look at the shooter, who was aiming at Gran, when a bullet took her down. Someone shot the gun out of her hand. She grabbed it up with her other hand, and was gonna shoot Gran, when someone grabbed her from behind and around the neck with one hand, and the gun hand with the other, got a pressure point, and made her let go and drop it. She was fighting like mad to get loose. The police and ambulance got there together. Sophie was still unconscious, and Gran had gotten the sling and the baby off of her. She prayed Ezekiel 16:6 and had gotten the bleeding stopped. She had taken a clean white handkerchief and put it on the side of Sophie's head. When the two ambulances got there, Gran moved away and sat on the steps. She got Abby Grace calmed down and checked over by one of the EMTs. She called Granddad and asked if Jim was there at the office.

He said, "Yes. Grace, what's wrong?"

She said, "Get Jim and drive him to the hospital, Sophie's been hurt.

"I will meet you there."

"Get started, and once you are on the way, call me and put me on speaker phone, and I will tell you what happened."

Granddad said, "Grace, are you injured?"

She said, "No, I'm just shaken really good. I will be fine." Her voice didn't give him any assurances.

Granddad grabbed Clifton, a realtor at their firm who wasn't busy at the moment, and said, "Come on, I need you to take over for Jim. We have a family emergency." When they walked into Jim's office, the look on Granddad's face said something was wrong. Granddad looked at Jim's client and said, "We have a family emergency and have to leave. Clifton here will take care of you."

"Go," the man said. And they did.

Jim was saying, "What's wrong, Granddad? Is it Gran or Sophie?"

"It's Sophie," Granddad said. "Here, call your Gran. She is gonna tell us, put it on speaker phone."

Jim thought his heart would stop before Gran answered. "Please, Gran, what's wrong with Sophie?"

Gran was crying and said, "A woman grazed her head with a bullet when we walked out of the restaurant. It's just a graze, but she hit her head on the brick steps when she fell. She was still unconscious when the ambulance left for the hospital with her. Let's pray," and they all did; and had been.

Jim said, "Where is Abby Grace? Is she all right?"

"Yes," Gran said. "She is in the car seat. We are in my car. I'm arriving at the hospital now."

"And we are almost there," Granddad said. "Wait for us."

"I will," she said. "I'm parked in the front parking lot." Jim and Granddad turned sick when they saw the blood splattered all over Gran. She wasn't even aware of it. She had cried and prayed till her eyes were swollen, and she was hoarse.

"We are here," Granddad said. Gran could hear Jim crying and calling out to God. They hurried to Gran's car as she was getting Abby Grace out of her car seat. She noticed Abby had blood on her, took some wipes, and was cleaning her up, when the guys walked over. Jim turned sick and weak in the knees. He almost went down.

Granddad wasn't doing well either at the sight of Gran with blood all over her. Jim saw the sling Sophie carried Abby in, and he really broke down. Jim got the car seat and Abby, Gran the diaper bag, and they all headed into the emergency department and asked about her.

The desk nurse said, "Dr. Robb is checking her over and will be out soon to talk to you." The nurse looked at Gran and said, "Are you injured?"

"No," she said, "just shaken."

"We can get someone to see you."

"No," Gran said, "I will be okay."

The nurse said, "Since you all are well, let's bring you all over here to sit. This is a well area." They thanked her and sat down. Abby Grace was sleeping, thankfully. As Gran filled them in, Jim was falling apart.

Granddad said, "Jim, you have got to get it together and be strong. Sophie's going to get through this."

He said, "How much more pain do these people want to inflict on her? This has got to stop! I've got to take her far from here so she can be safe."

CHAPTER 34

At that time, the doctor came to them and introduced himself. "I'm Dr. Robb," he said. "I just want to tell you her vitals are good. She is still unconscious, and she has a concussion. I have sent her for an MRI, and I will let you see her when she gets back to her cubicle. Then we will see what the MRI tells us." At that time, a detective arrived and was directed over to them. He introduced himself as Detective Lyle Harris from the police department.

He said, "I need to ask you all some questions." The doctor started to leave. The detective asked him to answer a couple of questions. He asked about her injuries and condition.

Dr. Robb told him the same thing, and said, "I've got to go."

"Of course," the detective said and thanked him. He looked to Gran and said, "Please give me every detail of what happened." She did, as Granddad used wipes to clean her up. All Jim could do was cry. Gran had called Pastor Cliff. He and his wife arrived, and she helped Granddad with cleaning up Grace with baby wipes, as she answered the detective's questions.

Mrs. Anne, the pastor's wife, said, "Grace, may I hold Abby Grace?" She had awakened, and Jim was still all to pieces, so Gran was holding her.

Gran said, "I need to change her."

The desk nurse said, "Hold on," and gave her a disposable pad to lay her on. Someone brought bottles of water and coffee to each of them. They accepted the offer. They were shaken to the core.

Jim said, "I feel helpless. I can't protect them, and I can't take any more. I'm getting them out of here, and far away."

Detective Harris said, "Let's get through this one day at a time. We have the shooter in custody. May I sit with you all, and see how Mrs. Nelson is doing before I go?"

"Of course," Granddad said. Pastor Cliff prayed, and in a few minutes, the doctor came and said, "You may see her now. The immediate family only."

Mrs. Anne said, "Let me hold Abby while you go in." Jim almost passed out when he saw Sophie. She was swollen, bruised, and had a black eye from where she hit the steps.

Gran said, "I don't know how Abby Grace kept from getting hurt. It had to be God." Then Gran remembered about the bird and told them, "If Sophie had not ducked the bird, she would have been shot in the face." Jim shuttered at that thought and cried even harder. "I know God sent the bird," Gran said, "or things would be much worse right now."

Jim pulled himself together and prayed, and he went to her side and kissed her and said, "Hey, angel, I know you're tired, but I need you to wake up now. I need to see those beautiful emerald eyes. Can you wake up for me now?" No response. "Sophie, please, sweetheart, open those beautiful eyes and talk to me. I need you, Sophie. It's time to wake up now." No response.

CHAPTER 35

Gran said, "I will be right back." The guys thought she was going to the restroom. She came back with Abby. Abby whimpered, and Sophie's hand moved a tiny bit. They all saw it. Gran laid Abby in the crook of Sophie's arm, and Abby started searching for the breast. Granddad stepped outside as Jim and Gran put Abby to the breast. It was hard because Sophie was lying flat on her back. A nurse came in. Sophie moved her arm around Abby but never opened her eyes.

The nurse said, "I think we can slowly raise her a little, that will help." Abby started crying, and Sophie's eyelashes fluttered, but she never opened her eyes. They got Abby in a position to nurse. She was hungry; they had her nurse both breasts. When they cradled Sophie's other arm around Abby Grace, Sophie's fingers moved.

Jim leaned down by her head and said, "Sophie, open those beautiful eyes, sweetheart." After Abby nursed and was filled, Jim was burping her. He motioned for the nurse and Gran to step out into the hall. He said, "What are we going to do? Abby is breastfeeding only."

The nurse said, "I can call over to the nursery and see if we can get a breast pump."

"That would be wonderful."

"I just hope she will take a bottle. If not, maybe you can work in shifts to bring her to the nurse."

Jim said, "I'm not leaving her. I don't know that she is safe even here, and I don't want to be away from Abby."

Gran said, "You stay with Sophie. I'm going to take Abby and go check on your Granddad."

"Okay," Jim said. He stood by Sophie's head and said, "Angel, I need you. Please open your eyes." He began to weep and to cry out to God, praying for her healing. He said, "Lord Jesus Christ, have mercy on your daughter." And he felt her hand go through his hair. He looked at her and said, "Oh, thank you, God. Oh, thank you, God."

Tears were streaming down her face, and his. She said, "I'm here."

He said, "And I'm so very thankful." He saw she was bewildered, and he said, "Everything is going to be fine. You just need some rest."

She clutched his arm and said, "Where is Abby and Gran?"

"They are here and okay."

She put her hand to her head and said, "What happened? I was coming from lunch with Gran. I remember a bird flying toward me," and then she touched the bandage and said, "Did someone shoot me?"

"Yes," he said.

She said, "I want to see Gran and Abby."

"You shall." He pushed Gran's number, and she answered. He said, "Sophie's awake and wants to see you all."

"On our way. Praise God, thank you, Jesus."

The nurse saw them going in, smiling through tears, and knew there was some kind of progress. She came through the door and looked at Jim's glowing tear-streaked face, and said, "Why didn't you call me?"

He said, "I was so overjoyed. I couldn't think, and this is what she asked for."

The nurse said, "You, little lady, have had a rough day, and I need to get some vitals." She put her finger over her mouth. All Sophie's vitals were good, and she said, "I need to shine a light in your eyes, and I need you to keep them open. Okay?"

"Okay," Sophie said. She shook her head and said, "My head hurts and is really sore."

"I'm sure it does and is. But you are doing amazing. I want you to close your eyes and rest. We have a room for you. I'm going to let the doctor know that you are awake. He will be in to check on you, and then we will get you upstairs."

"No," Sophie said. "I need to go home."

"The doctor will be in." She put her finger on her mouth and looked at all of them as the door closed.

Sophie looked at Gran and said, "Did I get shot?"

"Yes, but God sent a bird, and you ducked, and it just grazed your head. But it caused you to fall and hit your head."

Sophie said, "I was holding Abby Grace."

"And Jesus protected her, and she is fine."

Sophie looked up and said, "Thank you, thank you, thank you."

They all said, "Yes, thank you."

The doctor came in and said, "Well, we are so glad to see those eyes open. I'm Dr Robb. He had her squeeze both his hands and asked her where her pain was.

She said, "My forehead, on the right side, and the back of my head."

He said, "Are you in pain anywhere else?"

She said, "My back and shoulders are really sore."

He said, "May I look?"

She said yes. And he raised the bed a little more.

He said, "Does your lower back hurt?"

She said, "No." He looked at her back and had her shrug her shoulders.

She could, so he said, "You will be sore, but if you have any different symptoms, let us know."

She said, "I need to go home."

"I understand that," he said, "but I must keep you a couple of days. You have a concussion." Tears started falling, and he took her hand and said, "It is my responsibility to take care of you. Please trust me to do that, and rest. We will arrange for you to pump milk, and your family can bring your beautiful little girl here for you to nurse her tomorrow. It's going to be all right."

She said, "I need to be with my baby."

"I understand that," he said, "but you have some serious injuries and other complications that could get worse. We need you here for you to rest, and for us to be here if your condition worsens." She started crying; so did Jim. The doctor said, "Sophie, I have a daughter your age, and if she was in this bed, I would not let her go home. I have to do all I know to keep you doing well. Trust your family and your God to take care of you here and your baby there with them." Sophie nodded, and it hurt. The breast pump came, and he said, "I'm going to allow the nurse to assist you in pumping milk and then you will go into ICU so we can keep a close eye on you. After I check you in the morning, we will see whether to move you to a regular room." She started to protest, and he said, "Don't. Now I'm going to let your family pray with you and say good night, and they will see you in the morning. Rest in the promises of your God."

CHAPTER 36

As the Nelsons came from Sophie's room, Dr. Robb motioned for them to come to the other side of the hall, and said, "God has worked a miracle that she is awake. She has a bad concussion and is going to need lots of rest to heal. We need to put her first." They all listened intently. He said to Jim, "I know you want to be here, but if you walk into that room, it's going to stimulate her and affect her rest, so for her, I want you to go home and rest and be there for your baby. When that baby wakes up, she needs you. I will have them pump breast milk in four hours between now and then please rest. You all need rest." They all nodded and thanked him. He said, "If there are any changes, the ICU will notify me, and I will call you." It was so very hard for Jim to walk away. They assured him they would keep a close eye on her and that she would be safe. The transport nurses came and took her to ICU.

They said, "She will be in room 3."

"Thank you," Dr. Robb replied, with his finger on his lips. Sophie never opened her eyes. The doctor said good night, and they returned to the ER waiting room where the pastor, Ms. Anne, and Detective Harris waited. They filled them in, and after prayers, they picked up some dinner. They went by Jim and Sophie's to pack a bag for the two of them. It was seven thirty when they got home to Granddad and Gran's. Jim insisted on Abby Grace being in the room with him, and Abby took the bottle okay but was fussy. Gran gave her a good warm soak in her long sink she used for canning on the other side of the kitchen. Abby loved the long warm bath.

Jim said, "She is going to wrinkle if you leave her in there any longer."

Gran said, "I'm worried that she will be very sore after that fall today. Should we have had her checked? An EMT checked her at the scene, and I've checked her over well, and I don't see any swelling or bruising anywhere, and she is moving all of her body parts well. That's why the long bath. I want to get the soreness out and make sure she is still moving well. The Lord really protected us all today. It's a miracle we are not all dead. She turned the gun straight at me as I was getting Abby Grace. Someone grabbed her from behind and stopped her from killing me."

"I'm so very thankful," Granddad said from behind her.

"Me too," Jim said.

"Me three," Gran said. "It's gonna take all three of us to keep this one occupied. I know she is wondering where her mommy is, and I pray she takes the bottle. She did after her bath. She was so hungry." Gran put a tat of rice cereal in the bottle, and she took it and went to sleep. They all prayed and went to bed by nine o'clock. Jim had called the girls and filled them in and told them that they would not be allowed to see her yet. He asked them to thank God for what He had done, to keep praying, and he would update them in the morning. They called the prayer chain at their church and got some warriors on their knees. Jim wanted to be at the hospital early to get milk for Abby and to check on Sophie. Abby Grace was up at two in the morning, fussy and wanting Mama. Gran heard her, and by the time Jim diapered Abby and got to the kitchen, Gran had her bottle ready. She was hungry but wanted Mama. She finally settled down and took the bottle, then went to sleep. They were all exhausted; it had been a difficult day. Jim had trouble going back to sleep. He missed Sophie being beside him, and he was so worried about her. He prayed himself to sleep.

CHAPTER 37

Abby was up at six thirty, wet and hungry, and looking for Mama. She fought the bottle but finally took it because she was hungry. Jim left her with Gran and was headed for the hospital by seven thirty. They wouldn't let him in but told him they expected her doctor soon, and they had breast milk. Someone from the nursery had helped her pump and bottle milk for him. He called Lauren, their office assistant, and she came up to the waiting room so he wouldn't miss the doctor. The nurse brought the milk out to Jim. He gave it to Lauren and said, "I need you to take this straight to Gran at home." He handed her $20 and said, "Here's some gas money."

She said no.

He said, "Yes, now go, and thank you so very much. I know it's not in your job description."

She said, "It is. I'm there to assist in any way I can. I pray for good news." He thanked her again, and she left.

Jim called Gran and said, "Lauren is bringing the milk. I'm having to wait until after the doctor sees her before I can go in. I will be home after I see her."

Jim was sitting there praying when the doctor came out and said, "Mr. Nelson, your wife is much improved."

"Thank you, Lord," Jim said.

Dr. Robb said, "Yes, thank you, Lord."

Jim said, "Is she going to get out of the ICU today?"

"I think I'd like to keep her at least until the morning. She really wants to see you and her baby. I told her you were here, and I would let her see you soon. And if she rests well, and does well, that you may bring the baby this afternoon and let her nurse. But only once though. Her concussion is serious, and I must take the best of care for her."

"Yes, please do."

Dr. Robb said, "I'm going to let you see her now. Don't ask her questions or overstimulate her mind. We need her calm and restful. Tell her you will be back later to let her nurse the baby. They just came from the maternity ward to help her pump milk. They should be finished. You may go see her now for fifteen minutes."

"Thank you so much."

"Remember, don't say anything that would upset her or over-stimulate her."

Jim said, "I want her well and home. I will be on my best behavior." When Jim went in, Sophie felt his presence and opened her eyes. "Hello, beautiful."

"Hi," she said. "My, you are a sight for sore eyes." She gave him a big smile and winced in pain.

He said, "Your head is really sore, isn't it?"

"Yes," she said, "it is. I need to see Abby Grace. Is she all right?"

"Yes, and she wants to see you." The doctor said I can bring her this afternoon." He said, "He wants you to rest after our visit."

Sophie said, "I want to go home."

"I know," he said, "and you will, but not today. It is too soon. You have to heal." Tears rolled down her face, and he kissed them away and said, "Darling, if it was me in this bed, you'd want me to follow all the doctor's advice and get well."

"Yes," she said, "so, okay, I will behave."

"Good," he said. "I miss you." At the end of their visit, he kissed her and said, "Rest, I will be back with Abby in a while." She closed her eyes and fell asleep as he prayed over her. At two thirty, Jim brought Abby because he knew she would be ready to nurse. She was. She was all smiles for her mommy. She nursed both breasts and slept by her mother's side. Jim sat quietly, praying, and the nurse let them stay about forty-five minutes before she shooed them out. She told Jim that she would leave a note with the next charge nurse that he could visit for twenty minutes at eight o'clock and pick up milk at the nurse's station.

She said, "Then eight in the morning, okay?"

"Yes," he said. "Thank you." He took pictures of Abby Grace that afternoon so he could show Sophie when he went back at eight. Sophie was much improved and wanted out of there. Jim said, "Rest and relax so your head can heal, and you will be out of here soon."

Sophie said, "I'm tired of resting."

"I know, sweetheart, but your body is not going to properly heal without it. You fell and hit your head hard, and we want you well. Please be patient."

"I will try." She saw his concern. When he kissed her good night, she said, "I don't want to let you go."

"I will be back in the morning."

CHAPTER 38

She was glad to see him when the morning came. Dr. Robb was in at seven. When Jim got there at eight, they let him come back. The charge nurse told him they were going to move her out of ICU. She said, "You may see her in fifteen minutes. We are going to move her probably about nine, and that will exhaust her. You may bring the baby to nurse about eleven thirty. She doesn't need a lot of company. We have to let her rest in between feedings, okay?"

"Yes, okay. I want her well." The detective had wanted to talk to her, and they wouldn't let him.

He called Jim and asked about her. Jim said, "She never saw it coming. She doesn't know why a woman would want to shoot her."

Detective Jones said, "She was dating Sophie's ex when he died, and apparently held your wife responsible for his death."

"Oh," Jim said.

"I know it doesn't make sense to you and me, but some people have a twisted sense of right and wrong."

"Amen," Jim said. Then he said, "I don't know if I will ever feel she is safe here." At eleven thirty, Jim brought Abby. Sophie turned on her side and nursed Abby. Then he moved Abby as Sophie turned to the other side. Abby was wailing. She wasn't ready to stop nursing or leave her mother. As Jim placed her back in Sophie's arms, she stopped crying and was searching. She nursed, then slept. Jim picked her up and stayed another twenty minutes, then took Abby home and brought her back at six thirty. She was so happy to see her mother. She nursed both breasts, and they took home milk she had pumped in between their visit. Jim kissed her goodnight at seven twenty and said, "We will be back in the morning."

As they were leaving, Connie and Debbie came in, and each had to hold Abby a few minutes. They promised to only stay a few minutes. Jim stayed with them, and they all left at seven thirty-five. Everyone slept better that night. As Jim came in the next morning, Gran and Granddad came with him and Abby. Sophie was all smiles. She said, "The doctor said maybe I can go home in the morning."

"Great," they all chorused. "We are ready to get you home." Abby was happy and making little squeals, which they all enjoyed. Granddad went to work for a while. Jim, Gran, and Abby left for her to get some rest. They were back at eleven thirty to twelve thirty, then five until eight thirty. Jim watched a movie with her and kissed her good night after Abby nursed again. Jim was thanking God for the miracles He had performed. If God had not intervened, He would have lost the two most important women in his life, and his precious baby girl. He felt he, nor Granddad, could have survived that.

CHAPTER 39

Going home. Sophie called early and said, "I need clothes to wear home."

"Awesome," he said, "be there in thirty." She nursed a hungry baby, and she dressed to go with the nurse checking her well to make sure she wasn't experiencing any dizziness or nausea. She had a little bit but wouldn't own up to it. She was ready to go home. When Jim passed their driveway, she said, "I want to go home."

"I know," he said. "I feel we need to stay at Granddad and Gran's a few days till you are stronger." He knew in his heart that it would be a battle to get her not to go back home. He was going to have to put his foot down and tell her no. She would be heartbroken, but he could not risk any of their lives anymore. She had no idea that Freida was going to kill Gran too. Jim had to face the fact that those people seriously wanted her dead. He had to find a way to help her see that. He and Granddad were already looking at a place on the other side of the lake, and she could still go to the sanctuary. None of Gregory's friends ever knew of it. Jim and his grandparents had talked to Connie and Debbie, who were in agreement they were never to go back there.

Connie and Debbie came to dinner that evening and were so glad to put eyes on Sophie again. She was doing well, and they were dreading the fight that would be coming in a few days. Jim worked from his grandparents' home, so he could be there with Sophie, Abby, and Gran. They all prayed for Father God to give them wisdom when the argument came. Jim and Granddad had gone the night before she left the hospital and gathered everything they could think of that they might need. In the afternoon of her second day home, she wanted to go to the sanctuary. Jim said okay, and he told Gran they were gonna drive back to the sanctuary and take Abby. Sophie said, "I wanted to walk," and he said, "We will drive part of the way, and walk the rest. It's too soon for you to overexert yourself."

"That's right, dear," Gran said. "Now go and have a great time," and she handed them bottles of water. Sophie smiled and kissed her cheek. It did her good to get out. She prayed and thanked God for sparing their lives. She asked for strength for the rest of her life and journey, and for God to give them wisdom in their marriage and the raising of Abby and any other children they might have. She thanked God again for sparing their lives, and as she and Jim got up, she felt so much lighter, and so did Jim.

The next afternoon, as Jim came from working in the den, Sophie said, "Let's run over to the house and get some things."

He said, "Could it wait till tomorrow? I wanted to take you for a drive."

Gran said, "Let me watch Abby Grace, and you two go have a nice ride."

"Where are we going?"

"Just for a short ride to get you out."

Sophie said to Gran, "But you have dinner to make."

Gran said, "She can stay in the kitchen with me, and I will talk to her." As she leaned down to pick her up, Abby squealed in delight. She was learning to make noises and loving it.

As Jim went out of the driveway in the opposite direction, Sophie asked, "Where are we going?"

"You will see in a moment." He held her hand and was praying, "Father give me the right words." As he pulled into a driveway less than a mile from Gran's, Sophie noticed it had a For Sale sign. He rarely showed her properties, maybe there was something he needed to do here. It was a lovely house, similar to theirs, but with updated landscaping. He got out, came around and opened her door, and said, "Let's go in for a few minutes." Still, she thought there was something he needed to do there.

As they went through the door, she said, "Wow, this place is beautiful. I love the colors and updates." She really loved the kitchen. It was laid out almost like hers. "Wow, someone is going to love this place!"

Jim breathed a sigh of relief. He said, "Walk on through, it's got great updated bathrooms."

"Wow, this place is beautiful all through."

He said, "The sanctuary is just right up there, and Kelly and Ahna live right out there."

Sophie said, "Someone is going to be very happy here."

Jim said, "I was hoping we could." And he heard the wind go out of her, and her hands went over her face, and she fell apart. Jim said, "Sophie, we can't go back home, it's too dangerous, for all of us. When you were shot, God sent a bird to save you and Abby and an off-duty police officer to save Gran. We can't take any more chances."

She said, "They tried to kill Gran too?"

"Yes. I don't know if they have connected the dots with Gran and Granddad. She was also with you when you two were run off the road. I worry about them too."

Sophie clung to him and said, "I had no idea when I came back here that I was bringing danger to anyone."

"We know," he said. "Sophie, we have to keep everyone safe."

She cried some more and said, "I need to go far away so all of you can be safe. It's my fault."

"No, stop it, Sophie. We are all in this together, and we are gonna make it together." Jim kissed her and said, "This handkerchief is drenched, you can't keep crying. Let's go home and rest, feed Abby Grace, and we can talk about it after. We need to keep you calm, sweetheart."

She squeezed him and said, "Let me walk through one more time," and as they did, she felt peace, and it felt like home. She put her arms around him and said, "You are so wonderful. I don't deserve you."

"Oh yes, Father God meant us for each other, and we are good for each other, and we will grow old together with a house full of kids and grandkids."

She said, "I like the sound of that. As soon as my head heals, we will work on growing the family."

He said, "Let's get settled in the new house first," and they both laughed and left. Jim loved hearing her laughter. He was thankful. The day she was shot, he wasn't sure he would hear it again.

CHAPTER 40

It took three weeks to get everything set up for the move. They needed security guards, officers, and off-duty officers to make sure everyone was safe and no one was watching. They even had off-duty officers guarding the lakefront and making sure no one was out there looking. Security was also walking the path in both directions. Officers also watched the road in both directions. It took all day, and by nightfall, everything was in place, and the beds were made. Granddad and Gran gathered them all in a circle before they left, and after a big prayer, they all said good night. They had moved on a Tuesday. They did not put up a mailbox. They had their mail sent to the office. They all got new vehicles and started coming home from the opposite direction. It was a mile further, but they adjusted quickly. It was a cold day at the end of January when they moved. One of Gran's friends brought them a pot of vegetable soup, corn muffins, fried apple pies, and a gallon of sweet tea for dinner. They were all stuffed and sent her a thank-you picture of all of them holding their tummies and smiling. They rested well in their new home.

They were torn as to what to do about the other one. Sophie would not get rid of it, even if she could. Luz brought dinner that second night; she knew their situation and asked what they were going to do. Sophie said, "I don't know. I can't let anyone live there, it's not safe."

Luz said, "It could be. Put a For Sale sign up on both sides, wait a few weeks, put a Sold sign on it. Leave it up a few weeks, then put Private Property signs, and Keep Out signs. Then add a generic name to the signs, and even put a mailbox with that name on it."

Sophie said, "But who would live in a situation like that?"

Luz said, "I know a family who would, and they are Hispanic like me, so anyone who might watch your house would believe you had sold it. Let my brother Joel, please, they will take good care of it."

Sophie said, "Luz, I couldn't live with myself if something happened to your brother and his family."

Luz said, "Trust me. We will walk that property over and anoint it. Our God will take care of them."

"Let me run it by Jim," Sophie said. "Okay? And I will let you know. It sounds good." Sophie gave her a big hug, and Luz went home to feed her family. Jim liked the idea and said he would draw up some paperwork. They both felt lighter with that burden lifted, and they rested wonderfully that night.

CHAPTER 41

Sophie missed her grandparents' home but enjoyed where she was. The walk to the sanctuary was about the same distance. On the weekends, they had game night on Saturdays with Connie, Debbie, Chris, and Jordan. The girls had chosen house plans, and construction was to start by the end of February; they should be moved to Mountain Lake by the first week of June. They each were confident there would be work for them in the area. Mountain Lake was growing, and more businesses were coming into the area. They all thanked God for His blessings daily—the seen and the unseen. Abby Grace was crawling, sitting up, and was one happy little girl. Sophie had her first children's book at the publisher, and was quite excited and working on her second. Jim was busy and working from the office most days. Ahna came for playdates two or three days a week in the afternoons. Abby loved her so very much.

Kelly met a wonderful man at the park. His two little girls were playing with Ahna, and they started talking. Josh was in the music ministry team at his church. He asked her and Ahna to join him and his girls for pizza. They were now dating. In April, they all got together for a big egg hunt at Jim and Sophie's house. They had a wonderful afternoon. The guys went bowling after the egg hunt. The girls sat and planned another wedding. Connie's was in June, Debbie's in July, and Sophie and Jim's anniversary was the end of August. They chose the third weekend in July to give everyone a break after Connie's wedding. Debbie chose a beautiful wedding gown. Her colors were soft pink and silvery gray. They did a great job of keeping the weddings simple. They both had moves coming up. Chris and Jordan's families were easy to work with. It felt good to have life feeling safe again. Frieda had taken a plea bargain, life in prison, instead of going to trial. They felt safe, but three days before Luz's brother was to move into the lake house, Jim dreamed it burned. He didn't tell Sophie, but he told Granddad.

He said, "It's a warning from God. I've felt uneasy for two days." They found them another place to move and didn't tell Sophie. Four days later, someone burned it to the ground. He set it with explosives all around. The fire department couldn't save it. It was under investigation. Evidence was found on the lakeside that tied it to Frieda's brother. Sophie cried for days and wouldn't leave the house.

She said, "It's never going to end. We are never going to be safe." Jim was feeling the same way.

He said, "Granddad, I don't know that you and Gran are safe. They will connect the dots. Some of those guys will be out of prison in just a matter of years, and no one will be safe."

Granddad said, "Let's take a getaway this weekend. We need to look at somewhere to retire, and as I was praying, a place came to mind. We can all drop off the grid." He and Gran knew none of them were safe anymore. They had discussed it several times, knowing they needed to move, but they had so many memories here. The bad ones were adding up. They did not want memories of lost loved ones because they refused to move. They took a vacation to the Nashville area. Then went to the Pigeon Forge area, and a little ways out, they found a farm they loved. They loved the area, and it had a lot of opportunities for growth for all of them. The farm was 160 acres. Sophie could continue to write under another name. They each changed their last name to Gran's maiden name, Sanders. Granddad had sold the business and told them they were moving to Dallas, Texas, to retire, and that they had family there. They asked Luz and her family if they wanted to move there too, but they chose not to because of their extended family. Jordan and Chris didn't want to leave. No one moved till after Connie and Debbie's weddings. Everything went smoothly. The girls got new cars again and changed their hairstyles and color.

Four months after the move, Jim and Sophie decided to have another baby, and she was pregnant immediately. They were overjoyed to find out a little boy was on the way. Daniel Isaiah came into the world hungry, and seven pounds, fourteen ounces, a very handsome fella like his dad. Sophie and Jim felt blessed beyond measure. The move had been good for them. All their business investments were doing well. God was blessing everything they put their hand to because they honored Him with their lives, and money, realizing that, as the Word says, "it all belongs to God our creator." They had a late Thanksgiving with Connie, Jordan, Chris, and Debbie. Debbie was just starting to show, and just found out it was a boy. They were partial to the name Samuel and wanted a biblical middle name. They liked Isaiah and wondered if it would bother Sophie and Jim if they used the name.

"Of course not," they both said. Connie announced they were going to try in January.

Sophie said, "I like having lots of babies around." They all agreed. Abby Grace was talking up a storm and loving her brother.

CHAPTER 42

Life was sweet. They all felt happy and at ease in Tennessee. They were glad they had moved. Gran loved having Granddad home every day. They loved their farmhouse and added their own special touches. They grew a garden and went down to their local farmers market on Saturdays and sold extra produce. They watched Abby in the mornings for a couple of hours so Sophie could write. Isaiah still slept a lot. Sophie and the children spent time on the screened porch in the afternoons. Sophie got some good writing done, then both of them napped on the porch. They all walked in the evenings. Late summer, they all peeled and sliced apples to dry and made apple butter. Their trees had an abundance of apples that year. Sophie and the ladies, in the Bible study she attended, had contacts with the women's shelter, area schools, and knew where to take their extra produce and fruit. The farm stretched out long ways. Jim had never taken Sophie to the back of the property.

On their wedding anniversary, Gran had made them a special dinner. To Sophie's surprise, the girls were there. Luz and Kelly helped. After dinner, Jim asked her to walk with him. "I found a special spot on the back of the property I want to show you." She asked if anyone wanted to join, and everyone was too full. They made small talk, pointed out pretty spots along the way. Then they rounded a curve, and he heard her gasp, and she fell apart. He caught her in his arms, and she squeezed him till he could hardly breathe.

"Thank you," she said. "You are the best. I can't believe you did this. How?"

He said, "Granddad and I have been working hard to get this done by today, and Kelly cleaned it up for us." There were beautiful flowers, flowering bushes planted all around, and a wooden bench off to the side, a sign saying Happy Anniversary. She was crying till she could barely see. It was beautiful. Her very own little sanctuary.

She said, "Every time I think I couldn't possibly love you more, you amaze me again. I'm the luckiest, happiest woman in the world to have you as the love of my life." She had already soaked his hanky and shirt, and needed those Kleenex inside. She said, "How did you get the wood so close to the same?"

"We bought old barn wood."

She cried and said, "You two are amazing, and the best. This is the best gift ever." They prayed and thanked God for His blessings, and as they got up, she kissed him till he tingled. She heard Abby talking and said, "We've got company."

"Yes, we do," he said. As they came out, there was a crowd. Their pastor and his wife were there from Mountain Lake. More flowers—Sophie was looking in awe, and Jim dropped to his knee as cameras went wild.

Sophie said, "What are you doing?"

"Asking you, will you do it again? A vow renewal at our new sanctuary on our anniversary."

"Yes!" she screamed. "Yes!" And they did. Sophie was dehydrated from crying all those happy tears, and they were all exhausted after. When they got back to Gran's, Karen turned on the music.

Jim said, "May I have this dance?" Through tears, they danced to "I Wanna Be Loved."

She kissed him and said, "I'm the luckiest woman alive. I am so loved, and I love you so very much." Then she ran to Granddad's arms, thanked him, and then Gran.

Gran said, "One more thing."

Sophie said, "What more could we possibly need?"

Luz and Armando said, "Cake," and stepped aside to show replicas of their wedding and groom's cakes. Tears poured again. It was an anniversary beyond belief.

Sophie said, "I feel like the happiest, most blessed woman alive. I feel so loved."

She and Jim showed them their house plans for the new house and said, "Then we will have a guest house here." They had the most wonderful evening with dancing and fellowship. Everyone took cake with them. By ten o'clock, everyone had said good night, and Jim and Sophie put their sleeping babies to bed. Sophie showed her husband he was appreciated. She massaged his back, filled the big massage tub with hot water and a sweet fragrance, and turned on their wedding songs.

CHAPTER 43

Everyone adapted to life on the farm. In spring, they got sheep, donkeys, cows, goats, and chickens. Soon they had baby goats; black and white. Abby thought there was nothing more beautiful. Then Granddad found two small peacocks and brought them home. They found two families in the church who were knowledgeable in farm animals and how to care for them. They built them houses. They bought two golf carts where they could run around the farm and take care of the animals. They lived on the back sixty acres and grew corn, hay, and large vegetable gardens. They were great people and loved it out on the farm. Sophie's books were selling great. Her third one was almost ready. She was enjoying the success. She was always invited to appear on talk shows but always declined, saying she was too busy as a mother and wife. She used a cartoon drawing of a mother and kids on the back of her book, instead of a picture. She weaned Isaiah at fifteen months, and three months later was ready for another one.

Connie and Jordan had a baby girl. Her beautiful red hair was a more vibrant shade than her mother's. She had Jordan's brown eyes instead of Connie's blue ones. They named her Beverly Anne, after her grandmothers. Sophie said, "I feel another book coming with a redhead in it." Father God had blessed beyond measure. They all loved getting together and letting the kids play. Jim and Sophie's new house had a big playroom. It was safe, fun, and had walls covered with pictures. Baby three was another girl. Sophie's mother was Sarah Elizabeth. Jim's mother was Mary Katherine. They chose between Katherine and Elizabeth and had the difficult decision of which to call her. They finally chose Katherine. Sophie and Jim walked their children and their dogs every day to the sanctuary when the weather would allow them. Gran and Granddad walked there early in the morning. They loved to start their days there.

When Katherine was fourteen months old, Sophie weaned her and said to Jim, "Let's have one more and see if we can get another boy."

He said, "I'm ready if you are," and ten months later, Jonathan David was born, a healthy 8.2-pound baby boy. All the kids loved him so very much. Jim said, "Children are a gift of the Lord, the fruit of the womb is a reward. Blessed is the man whose quiver is full. We are blessed, little mommy."

"Yes, we are," she said. Their barns were full. Their animals were fruitful. And they gave to their church, schools, and the community. Sophie had four best-selling children's books and was working on a six-book series. She tried to write two hours a day. Occasionally she got three hours. Karen had married and had twin boys. Luz and Armando were overjoyed.

Anna said, "Now I'm afraid to have children. I don't want two at a time."

They all laughed and said, "It's not likely that you'd have twins unless you date Luis's brother." She didn't say a word. They had been talking a lot lately. Chris and Debbie had two boys. Connie and Jordan had one of each. Life was getting busier, and they got together less.

CHAPTER 44

Abigail Grace was almost seven when, as they were finishing Bible study one night, she looked up and said, "I'm ready to ask Jesus in my heart. I want to do it now." Through tears, they asked her a few questions and knew she was ready. They prayed with her and wrote it in their Bibles' front cover, as she did hers. They heard sniffling, and looked and saw that Isaiah's lip was quivering.

He said, "I want Jesus in my heart, and He wants to come in." They all cried, and they led him to Jesus. They told him how proud they were of him.

"Let's go potty, then go tell Gran and Granddad the good news. Then we will take our walk to the sanctuary. They were so thankful for God's blessings and leading. Sophie rented a big cabin in the North Carolina mountains two weeks before Thanksgiving, for a week. They all went—Connie, Jordan, Chris, and Debbie. All had a wonderful time. They sang and danced and ate too much. It snowed, and they all thought it couldn't get much better. It was a grand week. Christmas movies, popcorn tins, snowballs, a snowman contest, Christmas cookies, and snow cream. It was amazing. The best Thanksgiving ever. Connie and Jordan and Chris and Debbie were staying a few days at the farm before heading back to Georgia. They all dreaded packing up and leaving; it had been an amazing week. Granddad's foot slipped as they were loading up the next day, and he fractured some ribs. They all wanted to stop and get him checked out. He wouldn't hear of it.

He said "I will see my doctor tomorrow. I will be fine till then." Gran insisted on driving. They put an ice pack on his side. He seemed fine. They all had dinner when they got unpacked. No one would let Granddad touch anything. They all ate at the guesthouse. They had ordered in. Granddad was moving slowly but insisted that he would be fine and would go to the doctor in the morning. They all had prayers before the grans said good night and walked across the yard.

Jim stepped out behind them and said, "Granddad, are you sure you're okay?"

He said, "Get back inside, I'm fine."

"Call me if you need me," Jim said. "I love you two."

"Back at you," they both said. Gran made him as comfortable as possible.

He said," I love you so much, Grace. I'm the luckiest man in the world to have won your heart."

She said, "There was no contest. You were the one for me, and I knew it." She eased carefully in bed beside him. They held hands and prayed. She said, "Wake me if you need anything."

They both said, "I love you," and held hands as they fell asleep. Gran awoke at four thirty and knew. She could barely breathe. She turned on the lamp and cried and cried. She pulled herself together after a while and called 911.

Then called Jim and said, "I need you to come over here."

He said, "Be there in minutes." He threw on some clothes and shoes quickly.

Sophie said, "What are you doing?"

"Gran needs me. Call me if you need me." They both knew something was wrong. Jim fell apart when he saw Gran's face. They held each other, crying, then Jim heard the ambulance coming. Sophie had a robe on and was there before the ambulance got in the driveway. She was bawling when she came in the door.

When she looked at them, she screamed, "No!" Jim and Gran both caught her. Everyone across the yard was awake by then and knew it had to be bad. Sophie was inconsolable. She loved Granddad so very much. Her heart was ripped in two for Gran. She held Gran and cried with her. She said, "I don't know what to do."

"Just keep holding me and praying." She did.

Jim said, "Make room for me in this huddle," tears streaming. He brought fresh handkerchiefs for each of them. They each scooted and put him in the middle.

Connie left Jordan with their kids and told Sophie, "I will go be with your kids and be praying for all of you." As she prayed for Father God to give them strength and help, she leaned down and kissed each of them on the head. "I'm so sorry," she said, bawling her eyes out, then she gave them all love. Debbie was there by then. She made coffee for Jim, and cups of tea for her, Gran, and Sophie. It was a difficult morning. Connie and Debbie made breakfast. They managed to get a few bites in Gran. Jim called the funeral home at nine o'clock. They went in at ten thirty and made arrangements. Gran told them they had discussed their deaths and wanted to be cremated and scattered.

Sophie said, "Can we do it at the sanctuary?"

"That would be perfect," Gran said. They had to wait on an autopsy. They planned the service for the next Sunday afternoon. It was a beautiful celebration of Granddad's life. They scattered his ashes all around as they sang "Because He Lives I Can Face Tomorrow," one of his favorite songs. It was a beautiful afternoon. They all sat till the sun was setting, telling stories of their time with Granddad, and what he had meant to them. He had impacted their lives more than he could have ever imagined. Father had given them an unseasonably warm day. The girls were smart enough to drive up in the Jeep and bring blankets. They all returned to Sophie and Jim's, and the church had brought an enormous amount of food—anything you could want. They all ate, and Gran did great, till it was time to go home.

Sophie said, "Abby wants you to stay with her tonight again."

Gran broke, and she stayed. "I will go home tomorrow night and be fine." The pastor and his wife, Edie, came by and visited the next morning. Edie gently said, "Ms. Grace, do you have someone to stay with you here? Or have you decided what you are going to do?"

"I am going to donate his clothing, shoes, coats, etcetera to the homeless shelter. I will look for someone to stay with me. This is home."

The pastor said, "Ms. Grace, I know someone who needs a place," and he shared that a college student who was in their congregation had been living with her grandmother and pursuing a writing career. "Her grandmother passed the day after your husband. She is about to be homeless. She is trustworthy."

"Bring her to me," Gran said. "This place will be great for her." When Alicia came, she and Gran bonded immediately. The place was perfect for her, and the sanctuary was her favorite writing place. She loved all the kids and animals. Alicia thanked Father daily for providing for her, and her writing was taking flight. She met her mate, Justin, at church. They dated ten months, and he asked her to marry him. Three months later, they married at the sanctuary. They moved to Nashville. Alicia had two books published and was working on a third.

CHAPTER 45

Alicia had found someone to stay with Gran. She had prayed for God to send someone very special, and He did. Amanda needed Gran desperately, and the two of them had a wonderful bond. She would drive Gran to the sanctuary in the mornings, and Gran taught her how to pray down heaven to earth. Three years later, Gran was sitting on the porch, watching the great grans play in the yard. Sophie was cutting up squash and okra to fry. Amanda was slicing the green tomatoes and onions. Sophie felt something stir in the air, tingles went over her. Gran looked in the direction of the sanctuary, and the most beautiful smile came on her face. It was as if years were erased, and Sophie heard her take her last breath. As Sophie reached for her phone, she heard Jim pull into the yard. He was an hour and a half early. Tears were streaming down all their faces.

The kids said, "What's wrong with Gran?"

Sophie put on a happy face and said, "Her spirit inside just went to be with Jesus and Granddad." Jim and Amanda watched as Sophie rejoiced with the children. She told them how Gran was with Granddad and Jesus and that she wasn't tired anymore. She and Granddad were dancing on streets of gold and having the most wonderful time. They were seeing their family and friends that were already there, and as Jim held her, the hearse came. They all cried. Sophie said, "Let me tell you why we are not gonna be sad. Gran has missed Granddad a long time, and as I was sitting here cutting okra, I felt the tingles of the spirit, and I looked up and saw that Gran had the most beautiful smile on her face. She was looking toward the sanctuary, and years of tiredness left her face. She just let her breath out here and caught it in heaven. She won't be here with us, and we will miss her, but we will all go to heaven when it's our time. Then we will be with them again forever. Now let's find something to eat."

She made dinner into a party. Jim said, "You were amazing."

Sophie said, "It was beautiful. I felt Granddad's presence as he came for her, and her smile when she saw him was so beautiful. I'm so sorry you missed it and so glad you showed up when you did. I needed your strength."

Jim said, "You're the strongest woman I know besides Gran."

"She taught me so much. There was no one like her."

Jim said, "You are. As we get older, we will be Gran and Granddad."

She said, "I hope we do as well. We all had great teachers." Jim and Sophie had Amanda read the kids a story and give them a snack so they could slip away to the sanctuary together. They knelt and prayed, thanking Father God for all His blessings. They reaffirmed their love and commitment to God and each other. They prayed that God would give them many years and help them to instill great values in all of their children. They told Amanda that she could stay with them till they found someone to stay in the house with her. Sophie waited and called everyone the next morning. Jim helped. They planned the memorial service at the sanctuary a week from Saturday, at two o'clock. It was beautiful. All the gang was there with their kids, all the houses were full. Connie, Jordan, and their two. Debbie, Chris, and their two. Kelly, Josh, and their three girls were all in the guesthouse. Alicia and Justin stayed at Gran's, along with Sophie's aunt Linda. Some cousins stayed there too. The place was lively. Food started arriving from the church and didn't stop. They didn't have to worry about a meal for over a week.

Aunt Linda was walking back with Sophie after the memorial service. Sophie noticed she was winded. She had actually noticed it a few times over the week. She asked her if she was okay. She smiled and said, "I'm very out of shape, and I've put on some weight. I thought maybe I could visit awhile and stay in the grans' house with Amanda."

Sophie said, "That would be perfectly wonderful, an answer to prayer."

Aunt Linda said, "It's so peaceful here."

"Yes, it is," Sophie said. Within a couple of weeks, Sophie realized Aunt Linda was not well. She had a moment alone with her on the porch a few days later. They were in the grans' rockers, having tea. Sophie reached over, held Aunt Linda's hand, and said, "I'm glad you came to stay with me. This is a peaceful place, even with so many kids and animals."

"It is," she said. "That's why I wanted to spend my last days here." She turned and looked Sophie in the eye. Tears were flowing down both their cheeks. "Is it okay if I spend my last days here?"

"Of course it is!" Sophie said. "I'm honored you want to be here. Do your children know?"

She broke down and said, "I don't know how to tell them."

"How long does the doctor think?"

"Three to six weeks."

"How about we plan a small reunion? We have room, and between now and then, we will pray Father will help us tell them."

"Thank you," Aunt Linda said. "You are such a wise woman."

"I've grown up under a few of them," Sophie said and squeezed her hand gently. Then said, "We need to plan a menu of what you and your family love to eat," and they did. Fall was coming. They had just built a new barn, so they planned the reunion in the barn and prayed for a beautiful warm day. It was three weeks out. Sophie kept it simple so as not to exhaust Aunt Linda. She had it catered. Connie and Debbie came but left their husbands and children at home. They were giving Aunt Linda good nourishment and lots of love. Debbie trimmed her hair two days before the reunion, and Connie did her nails and toenails. Aunt Linda rested and was ready for the big day, but she tired out quickly. After lunch, and an hour of fellowship, she said, "I need a nap. I'm going to lie down for a while."

Her kids looked at her, concerned, and Sophie said, "Let me drive you back to the house."

She said, "Sophie, will you help me after I rest? If you will just be there silently praying, it will give me strength."

"Of course I will. You lie down and rest. Call me when you are ready. I will show them around the farm."

Sophie said, "Farm tour! Come on, kids." They had a great time on the farm, and it kept them too busy to ask questions. Sophie caught Jim and told him the plan and asked him to keep up with all the kids and company. Connie and Debbie will help. Jim held her and prayed over her for strength for each of them. She thanked him. When Aunt Linda called her, the girls headed to Gran's to make tea and pray over Aunt Linda. It was difficult and painful. Sophie slipped out and gave them privacy after. Jim came and held her and gave her a good back rub as she cried.

"The next few weeks may get very rough," she said.

"I'm here for you," Jim said, "and we will get through this together. Our Father is with us all."

"Yes, He is. We would never make it without him." Aunt Linda slipped peacefully into eternity two weeks later, with her children and grandchildren around the bed. They were playing her favorite hymns and singing along as she took her heavenly flight. There was such a sweet peace in the room. She asked if she could have her ashes scattered at the sanctuary.

She said, "It's such a wonderful and peaceful place." They all agreed.

Sophie said, "Who will stay at Gran's with Amanda now?"

Kelly and Josh heard her and said, "We want to build a new house. Can we stay here while our house and barn are being built?"

"Sure," Jim and Sophie said. That took eleven months, and Amanda had found her Mr. Right. His name was Devon. They married and lived in Grans' house three years before his job took them to Chattanooga. They rented to a young couple of newlyweds who needed someone to take them under their wing and teach them how to pray. As they were having a heated argument one day, Abby was walking through the yard and overhead the yelling.

She came and said, "Mama, you need to take Adam and Angie to the sanctuary." They made many trips to the sanctuary, grew in Jesus and in their relationship. His job took them to Miami. Once again, the grans' home needed a family.

CHAPTER 46

Abby, at thirteen, was an amazing little lady. She loved Jesus and was her mama's right arm. She also found her mother's love for writing, trying to fit in an hour a day. She loved reading, especially love stories. Sophie found her a series of Christian love stories for early teens. She would talk to Abby about the greatest love story of all time. Sophie taught middle and high school girls in Sunday school. She taught sex education God's way, using the Word of God, teaching them that we are the bride of Christ. As Romans 12:1–2 teaches, we should present our bodies as a living sacrifice. Holy and acceptable unto the Lord. Next, she taught Proverbs 31. How King Lemuel respected and referred to His mother. Then they studied many love stories in the Bible. She wanted them to know who they were in Christ, and their value. Jesus went to the whipping post and the cross for each of us. He doesn't love one more than the other. We are all precious to him. Sophie and Jim both had a wonderful upbringing in the Word of God, and they made sure their children did as well. One afternoon, they asked Abby to watch her sister and brothers while they walked to the sanctuary. As they were walking back, they were talking about her beauty and maturity.

Jim said, "It's terrifying to think in the near future, I will have to get the shotgun ready. Less than three years, she will be ready to date."

"I've seen several boys at church looking her over. I have too, and she is looking back at Jonathan."

"Yes, she is. If I see her come in with his shirt on, the three of us are gonna have a family round table."

Sophie laughed and said, "Wouldn't that be something if history repeated itself?"

"Only the good part," Jim said.

"I pray none of them go through the heartaches we did."

"Amen! I sure wish Gran and Granddad were here to help us through the young adult years. We have four of them to get through. By the time it's Micah's turn, we will probably be grandparents."

"No doubt, Mr. Sanders."

"Yes, and one day we are gonna have to tell that story of our past. It wouldn't be good for them to find out on their own."

"No, it wouldn't, but I sure don't look forward to opening that can of worms!"

"Amen," Jim said.

CHAPTER 47

Pastor Tom introduced Jim and Sophie to Leah, a new church member with three small children. It was very evident Leah was a battered wife. Pastor Tom had talked to them ahead of time and told them of her need. Ms. Anne took the children a few feet away so they could still see their mama, and gave them some food. Jim and Sophie were with the youth pastor Clift, and his wife, Julia. Jim and Sophie said to Leah, "We understand that you and your children need a safe home, and we have one for you. You must understand that if you tell people where you are, you jeopardize our safety and our children's safety, so will you promise that you will not tell anyone your location?"

"Yes," she said. "I can't take it anymore. I have no money."

"You need no money! We have a safe place for you and your children."

Ms. Anne came over and said, "I will be out there in a couple of hours with the clothes and personal items you and the children need." Pastor asked his sister Pam to drive them out to the farm since she had their car seats in her van.

She said, "I'm gonna stop and feed them on the way."

"No need," Sophie said. "Lunch is ready at my house."

"Great," Pam said. "I will be right behind you."

They all prayed together, and Pastor Tom told Leah, "You are going to love where you are going, and so will your children." When Leah saw the name of the farm, she felt peace. Peaceful Acres farm. She absolutely loved the farmhouse. Sophie took her in while Jim and Abby got lunch on the table. Sophie showed them around the house, both of them with a baby on their hip. Leah had a one-year-old girl, a two-and-a-half-year-old boy, and a four-year-old boy. They were all shy and scared. They loved lunch, spaghetti and meatballs. The baby was falling asleep in the high chair. She let Sophie clean her and pick her up. Leah was shocked.

Sophie said, "She can feel the peace of God in me."

"I can too," Leah said. "We all can."

Sophie said, "Let's bed you all down for a rest before Ms. Anne gets here." They were exhausted. Jim had a crib up for her when they got back to the farmhouse. They got a one-hour nap before Ms. Anne arrived. Sophie had free and clear detergent and dryer sheets. She helped Leah wash all the new stuff. Sophie took her grocery order, then asked her, "What do you like to drink and snack on?"

She said, "I loved the hot tea, I don't need much."

Sophie said, "Here you can have your needs and wants." She reached over and held her hand and said, "You and your children are safe here. We are gonna help you."

Tears poured down Leah's cheeks, and she said, "I will never be able to repay you all."

Sophie said, "There will never be anything you need to repay. You keep us safe, and we will keep you safe. Now tell me what you want."

She said as tears rolled down her face, "I'd love to have some lotion, deodorant, and shampoo." Sophie realized how blessed she was. This precious battered sister did not even have the basics. Before Sophie left, she asked Leah what her favorite colors were. "Soft pink and soft blue," she said. When Sophie returned, she had soft pj's, a robe, and slippers. Leah cried.

Sophie held her and said, "It's an honor to do this for you. One day you will do it for others."

"I want to," Leah said.

"You will now stop that crying. Dinner is ready."

She said, "I can make something," as Sophie helped put the groceries away.

"Abby has dinner waiting for us. Let's go." They had a wonderful dinner, prayers, and Bible reading. Sophie and Abby helped them back across the yard. Sophie said, "This is your home. Leave on lights, do what makes you comfortable. Call me if you need me anytime of the night."

"Thank you, Sophie." They hugged, and Sophie walked across the yard, thanking God for His provisions for them all. She rested well knowing they were held in Jesus and she was wrapped up in her husband's arms.

CHAPTER 48

A new day

Leah woke up feeling so good and rested, and she had never owned a bed that felt so good. She felt like the farmhouse was a mansion. It was beautiful, clean, and so comfortable. She looked up to heaven and thanked God. She had no idea what she was going to do. She said to Sophie as they were having tea midmorning, "I have no car, no money, and three little ones to care for. I don't have a clue where or how to start."

"When you were in high school, what were your dreams?"

"I wanted to be a painter." She went in and got her purse and pulled a small notebook out, showed it to Sophie. The sketches were of her children, and they were amazing.

Sophie said, "Leah, you have an amazing talent. We are gonna help you bring it to life."

"How?" Leah said. Sophie pulled out her phone and looked up art supplies.

"I don't have money!"

"Your Father in heaven isn't broke. He said order $1,000 in supplies and get started."

Through tears, she did and said, "It may take years, but I will repay you."

"No, pay it forward," Sophie said.

"How will I sell artwork while I'm in hiding?"

"God has a plan for you. We will get a legal name change and sell your art under another name. God is going to provide you with all you need, and as He leads, you will give others a hand up."

Leah said, "I feel hope, and it feels so good."

Sophie said, "You have great talent and a reason to hope." Leah was so excited.

She thought for the first time in years, *I have hope, and I feel like I have a future.* She began to draw and paint as never before. Sophie asked Leah who she would like to be.

She said, "We will get a lawyer and get you a name change."

She thought for a few minutes and said, "I want to be Lydia Grace Martin."

"I like it," Sophie said. "It suits you."

"Thank you," Lydia said. "It's the grace of God that has set me free."

"Amen," Sophie said. "Get lots of art ready. When we get your new ID, I could take some of your work and show it to a friend who has an art studio." She agreed. Sophie took some to her friend Ruth Anne's studio.

Ruth Anne said, "Sophie, these are amazing. Did you paint these?"

"No. I have a friend, Lydia, who used to dabble to relax, and is now wondering if she might be able to do it for a living."

"Does she have more finished?"

"Yes!" Sophie said.

"Well, I have an artist retiring and will have some wall space right over here. Have Lydia drop by one morning between nine thirty and eleven."

"Will do," Sophie said, "and thank you."

"Thank you!" Ruth Anne said. Sophie could hardly wait to get home and tell Lydia. Lydia wept at the news. Her Father was answering the desires of her heart. She was going to make it. She and her children would be blessed. She had no idea how very much. As Lydia walked into the art studio, she felt a sense of peace. She had prayed the entire way. It was beautiful and very well set up. It would be amazing to have her artwork displayed here. She and Ruth Anne felt very at ease with one another. They went into the office. She opened her bag and uncovered the pieces she had brought with her. Ruth Anne said, "You are an extremely gifted young lady, and I will be very happy if you decide to display your art here. This is what I can do for you." As Ruth Anne described how her commission worked, and special events, Lydia was overwhelmed at what her Father had provided for her. Her art sold about as fast as she produced it. After dropping off art one day, she had other errands, so she stopped in a café next door for lunch.

CHAPTER 49

Lydia headed to a table. A man said, "May we share this table? It appears to be the last."

"Oh," she said. "Well, I could get mine to go."

"Nonsense," he said. "If we can share, I will buy your lunch."

He saw her eyes go to his ring finger, and he said "I'm a widow, two years now. Please," he said. She smiled and sat. "I'm Tom Meyer, a local." He held out his hand to shake, and as she touched his hand, she felt the Spirit of God in him. She looked into the kindest set of green eyes.

"I'm Lydia Martin, also a local."

Tom said, "I don't see a ring on your hand."

"I'm divorced," she said.

"I'm sorry you had to go through that." The waitress came and took their order.

Lydia said, "I haven't looked at the menu, but can I get a BLT with a large sweet tea?"

"Yes, make that two," Tom said. "Good ordering, little lady." She smiled, and his heart melted.

The waitress said, "Fries?"

"Yes," Tom said. Then apologized for jumping ahead of her.

"It's okay," she said. "No, I just want the sandwich and tea." They made small talk till the food arrived, and he thanked the waitress.

Tom looked at Lydia and said, "May I say grace?"

"Please," she said, and as he took her hands, she felt the Spirit in him. He thanked God for a new friend to share lunch with, for the food, and every blessing of life. Lydia was impressed and thanked him.

He said, "You have to try these fries. They are the best."

She took one and said, "You're right, they are amazing."

"Feel free to eat all you want."

"Thank you."

He said, "Do you have children?"

"Yes, three," she said. "And you?"

"I only have one. He left for college recently and is planning to go in the military. I'm so lonely without him."

"I'm sure that's very hard."

"The empty nest is painful for sure."

"I dread the thought of that," she said. "I've still got a while. Mine are two, three and a half, and five."

"Yep, you've got a while."

"I'm loving the journey. They are so sweet."

He said, "Children are wonderful. My wife and I could only have the one. We wanted more. We fostered a few, then when her cancer came back, it took her quickly." Tears rolled down his cheeks. He was embarrassed. She took his hand and prayed for him right there for peace, comfort, and healing.

She said, "It must have been terrible on your Stephen."

"Yes, it was. I think that's why he went away. Instead of going to a local college. He doesn't come home much. He says it's too hard to walk in and his mother's not there, so I visit him at college." He looked at her and said, "May I have your phone number? We could maybe share a meal again? It's great to have another Christian to talk to."

She said, "But I can't talk every day. I'm busy with three kids and work."

"I understand," he said. "May I give you my number, and you accept mine?"

"Okay," she said. I've got to get—oh my, I have a hair appointment. Thank you for lunch."

"Thank you," he said. "You blessed my day."

"Back at you," she said. He put money and a generous tip on the table.

He walked her out and said, "I will call in a couple of days, okay?" She smiled. He did too, and he watched her to her car. She felt giddy all over, not knowing he did too. Lydia decided that when she got her next check, she was going to get her a minivan. With the next one, put a down payment on a house. She was so excited. As she was thinking what to do first, she realized it was about time for her hair appointment. Her heart was singing. She had gotten her divorce before she had changed her and her children's names. She was so glad all that was done. She had really enjoyed lunch with Tom. He was quite a gentleman, and a Christian.

CHAPTER 50

Lydia felt ill at ease all of a sudden. She had a strange feeling as she walked into the department store to go to the salon. She had changed her hairstyle, color, and had lost twenty pounds with all the walking to the sanctuary she was doing. But her ex saw her straight in the face and thought that was her. He had seen her as she was going into the restaurant, as he was coming out. It was crowded everywhere. She didn't see him. Just as she got in her vehicle, Tom noticed a guy looking at her in a scary way. The guy pulled out after her. Tom took off after him and watched as he followed her into the department store at the mall. Tom followed him, and as he approached her, he grabbed her arm and clamped his hand over her mouth at the same time. He was dragging her backward. One lady took a picture as another called 911. Suddenly, as he was dragging her backward, he felt a gun in his back and heard the safety release. The gun was right behind his heart.

Tom said, "Let her go, or you'd better be ready to meet your Maker." Lydia recognized the voice. As her ex turned her loose, he pushed her down, ducked, and tried to kick her. Tom kicked his rear end with everything he had, and he went face-first in the carpet. The police arrived just in time to see it.

They cuffed him, and the other one told Tom, "Lay down your weapon." He had one hand in the air, leaned, and put his gun on the floor. The ladies were helping Lydia as she was crying her eyes out.

One of the ladies said, "I called 911." She had pictures. "We saw the whole thing. This man saved her, and can he at least shoot that monster in the butt before you haul him out? We will testify the gun accidentally went off."

"That's a very tempting offer, ma'am, but we shouldn't fire a gun inside."

She looked at Tom and said, "Shoot him in the butt when they take him outside."

He said, "I'd really like to." She saw his eyes were on Lydia. Lydia was so shaken. She was shaking so bad she could barely talk. Someone told them in the salon what was going on. Tina, Lydia's stylist, came out with a wet cloth. Tom was by her side, seeing if she was okay. He said, "Maybe we should take you to the clinic down the street and get you checked out, especially your knee, and get something for those carpet burns."

Lydia said, "How did you happen to be here?"

He said, "I followed you." As alarm came all in her face, he realized how that sounded, and said, "Oh, no, no, it's not what you are thinking. I was watching you to make sure you got safely to your car. I saw this guy watching you, and I didn't like the look on his face. He pulled out right behind you, so I pulled out behind him. He was walking in behind you. I'm sorry I couldn't get to you sooner and prevent this from happening. Is he your ex?"

"Yes, I'm afraid so. He must miss his punching bag."

Tom said, "I'm so sorry. Many men don't know how to appreciate a good woman." The two little ladies were keeping the officer busy while Tom talked to Lydia. Her ex started complaining, and one of them kicked him.

The officer said, "Ma'am, stay back please."

She said, "Oh, I'm sorry," and kicked him hard again. He was cursing.

The officer said, "Ma'am, step away and stop."

She said, "I'm sorry I couldn't get my leg high enough to reach his filthy mouth." He cussed her, and to his surprise, she slammed him in the mouth with her heavy pocketbook, busting his mouth.

Her friend was clapping, saying, "Way to go, Rosie."

The officer said, "Ma'am, go over there with your friend before I have to cuff you."

The ex said, "I'm suing you."

She laughed and said, "That will be a good front-page article. 'Wife beater and pervert gets beat up by a sixty-seven-year-old.' You want this bag back in your face?"

The other officer said, "Ms. Rosie, please come over here with me. I have more questions."

She came over to Lydia and said, "I'm sorry, hun. Are you okay?"

"I am, thank you, Ms. Rosie."

She said, "I whopped him good for you."

"You did," Lydia said "and thank you."

The officer finished his questions. Lydia said, "I need to go. I've got to get back to my children."

Tom said, "I'd feel better if you'd let me take you down to the walk-in clinic down the street."

"I will be fine. I'm used to pain and swelling."

She saw pain in his face, and he said, "Lydia that's not anything you should have had to endure. Men are not supposed to hit women and children." She was crying again.

The little women said, "He is right. Listen to him and marry him; he would treat you right."

He said, "I would."

Lydia looked at them, all embarrassed, and said, "I just met him today."

"That's all right," Rosie said. "It's all over his face. He cares for you."

"I do," he said. "She is a lovely lady who believes and belongs to God."

"Wow, you've got you a good one with good eyesight, outward and upward." Lydia stood and almost stumbled. Tom grabbed one arm, Rosie the other, and her friend Gabby had a hand behind her back. She thanked them all and started walking. They all followed. She forced herself to walk.

He said, "Please let me carry you home."

She said, "It's too far. Your arms will give out."

"I'd better drive." And they all laughed.

She leaned in, kissed his cheek, and said, "You are wonderful, and I want to get to know you. If you follow me home, you are gonna scare me."

He held up his hands and said, "Beautiful lady, that's the last thing I want to do. You've been through enough. I will call and check on you later this evening. Put some ice on your knee, and some over-the-counter pain meds will help. Do you need anything?"

She said, "I've got your number."

He smiled a dreamy smile, and Rosie said, "Do you have her number?"

"I do," he said.

Rosie said, "You'll be saying that before long."

"I hope so," he said. "She is amazing."

He kissed both ladies on the cheek, thanked them for getting involved and helping. He pulled out $50 for each of them and said, "Enjoy."

They both gave him a hug and said, "You already made our day. This was better than the soap operas." He laughed, blew them kisses, and went home.

CHAPTER 51

Lydia smiled through all the pain. She said, "Wow, Lord, all that was unexpected and could have turned out much worse if you had not let Tom see and follow. She prayed for all of her rescuers. Tom prayed for her, and for Rosie's foot. He knew it would be sore. She couldn't wait to tell Sophie. She called on her way home. She wasn't able to go to the grocery store.

Sophie said, "My gosh, are you okay?"

She said, "I will be. I will soak in the walk-in tub, then put ice on my knee."

Sophie said, "We know Tom. We bought goats from him. He is a nice man. He goes to church at In Him Baptist. I know several people who attend there. It's a great church."

Lydia said, "When he touched my hand to pray over lunch, I felt the Spirit."

"Tell me everything," Sophie said. They felt like giddy school girls. All of the kids were napping except Abby. She said she'd watch them while her mom helped Lydia with whatever she needed. She and Sophie had a good conversation. Sophie could tell she liked Tom and said, "When he calls and asks you out, say yes."

"What if he doesn't?"

"He will."

Lydia said, "I need to pray." They prayed, and Sophie gave her a glass of tea, something for pain, and made sure her phone was right beside her.

She said, "I will be back in thirty with an ice pack."

"Thank you," Lydia called out as Sophie walked away. Lydia was in a lot of pain and had a lot of soreness. Tom called every day.

He would say, "I know you are busy, but I just need to know how you are doing. I wanted to send you flowers, but I have no address."

She said, "You can't have it till I get to know you better."

"Okay," he said. "I respect that."

He said, "I know tomorrow is Sunday and you need your rest. I will call on Monday."

"Okay," she said. "Thank you."

He said, "You are in my thoughts and prayers."

She said, "And you're in mine."

"Till Monday, sweet lady." And he hung up. Lydia couldn't stop smiling. It felt so good to be genuinely cared for.

She thought, *I could get used to this, but could he handle my kids and the noise? I sure hope so.*

CHAPTER 52

Tom called Lydia, and she said yes to going out Friday night. Four months later, they married, and she moved in with him. His son, Stephen, took leave and came to the wedding. He was so happy to see his dad happy, and he loved Lydia and her kids. They were good kids.

Once again, Gran's home needed a family. Jim and Sophie prayed for God to send the right family, and of course he did. Their pastor called that next evening and said, "We've got a young couple in the church struggling. They have two small children. They are struggling in their marriage and their finances. I heard you have an empty house again. I'm not asking that you let them live there free. They just need lower than the $750 a month they pay now."

"Tell them you found them a house on a farm for $500 a month, utilities included. The kids will love the animals." A week later, Stuart and Hadley moved in with three-year-old Breanna and five-year-old Ashton. The kids loved the farm. They all did. The third night, Sophie saw they were out walking. They came out and asked if they wanted to walk to the back side of the hollow.

"It has a special spot. We go there daily."

"Sure," they said. They passed the barn, lots of trees, and two hayfields. As they rounded a bend, there was the beautiful little sanctuary. A little church.

Ashton said, "You have your own church?"

"My grandfather called it a little sanctuary."

"Wow!" they said.

Sophie said, "He had his own, and we walked there daily. He taught me how to pray and talk to God."

"Can you show me how?" Ashton said.

"If that's okay with your parents."

"Of course," they said. Jim, Stuart, and Hadley waited quietly at the door as Sophie and all the children knelt and prayed.

She kept it simple and explained, "As we begin to pray, at some point in time, God speaks to our heart. Then we ask him to come in. When we feel that, we ask Him to forgive us of our sins—things we say and do that we shouldn't have. Isaiah, give us an idea of what some sins are."

"Lying," he said.

"What's that?" Breanna said.

"It's like, if I take your toy, then I say I didn't do it. I would be lying. Or, if I'm playing at your house and I take something that is not mine, then that's stealing. God and His Son Jesus said that's sin and we have to say we're sorry."

Sophie said, "As we live and grow, we all do some things that we shouldn't, but our heart inside gives us a feeling that we need something, but it's really someone. It's Jesus we need. When you get a little older, you will understand. When He tugs at your heart, ask Him to forgive you, come live in your heart, and make it clean. Now let's pray." They did, and as she got up, all the adults were misty-eyed. She, Abby, and Isaiah had tears streaming down their faces.

Jim said, "You all are welcome to come to our special place anytime. My granddad and I built it not long before he passed away."

CHAPTER 53

Stuart and Hadley grew to love the sanctuary. They also grew in Christ and their love for each other. They learned a lot on the farm and loved living there. Abby had her fifteenth birthday. They celebrated on Saturday with Connie, Jordan, Chris, and Debbie, along with their children. They had a wonderful time, and the Georgia gang all headed home after lunch on Sunday. Sophie was in the kitchen, about to start a light dinner. Abby came in. Jim was close behind her, about to get a glass of water. He heard Abby say, "Mama, why do we never go visit any of them in Georgia? They always come here, meet them places, but not Georgia? I was born there."

Sophie looked at her, trying to find the words. She saw Jim had heard and, like her, was trying to find the right words. Sophie said, "Let's sit."

Abby saw her dad was there, and said, "Is it bad?"

"Yes," Sophie said. "We had to leave Georgia because our lives were in danger."

"Why?" Abby asked. "Who would want to hurt either of you?" Jim could see Sophie was struggling, yet he knew she had to tell this. He was praying Father God would give them both the words and the strength to tell their story.

She said, "Abby, I don't know that we can tell you everything today, it's a lot, but I promise you I will tell you everything. I was married before I married your dad. I was young, lonely, and my grandmother Stewart had just passed. A guy came to buy her car. Then he asked me out. I wasn't dating anyone at the time. He was handsome and charming, and I thought I was in love. Boy was I wrong. We need to date someone long enough to really get to know them. He was a very dishonest person. I ran him off and divorced him. He had stolen so much from me and all of my gran's valuable things. He came back to my house one day and was arguing with me, screaming at me in my yard." Sophie was crying. Jim came and stood beside her, gave her tissues, and held her from the side. "My neighbor called the police. He ran and got in his car, and as he pulled out in front of the police, one police car pursued him. The other stopped to assist me and find out what was going on. As my ex tried to outrun the police, he lost control of the car, hit a tree, and died at the scene of the accident. Because he had been arguing with me before he died, his brother and his girlfriend blamed me for his death. It wasn't my fault, but they want me dead. They tried a few times to kill me. They all went to prison but are probably going to get paroled in a few years, so we stay away from Georgia."

"Did they try to kill Dad too?"

"Yes, all of us. So you must never get on line and poke around. You could draw them to us. We have beautiful memories of Georgia. We grew up there. We married there, and you were born there. We must not go back though. None of us would be safe. I knew this day would come, and I've been dreading it."

Abby said, "I don't understand how anyone could hate you two."

"Look at the world, Abby. People hate others daily because of the color of their skin, or where they are from in the world. We are called to be like Jesus and love everyone. It's hard sometimes, but Jesus will help us. He said He would never put more on us than we could bear."

CHAPTER 54

As they were hearing footsteps coming, Jim squeezed them together in a hug and kissed them both on the head. "We are being invaded by the hungry mob. The movie is over." Sophie gave them some chips, Isaiah got them all a drink, and Sophie, Jim, and Abby made sandwiches. They ate, laughed, and talked about the movie. After dinner, they did their Bible study, got baths and showers. Abby didn't ask any more questions, for which Sophie was thankful. Jim was double-checking the doors and checking on all the kids. Sophie decided to fill the big tub. It had been a trying day. As Jim came into the bedroom, he heard the tub filling and the music come on. He knew he was a blessed man. She seemed to always know when he needed a little extra attention, despite the relaxing bath. Sophie had nightmares that night. Jim comforted her, prayed over her, and massaged her back as he prayed blessings over her. They fell back asleep in each other's arms.

They awakened to a new day, with a sweet little girl crawling up into their bed, saying, "Mommy, I'm hungry. It's time to get up."

They snuggled her, kissed her little face, and said, "Well, we had thirty more minutes till the clock says good morning."

"I'm hungry, Mommy."

"Okay, let's go see what we can find for breakfast." Jim got up with them. After they all pottied and washed their hands, they made breakfast, then headed to school after their morning prayers. Sophie came back after a run through the store. Jim had decided to work from home today. When Sophie got in the garage, he helped her bring in the groceries.

He said, "Your tea is ready."

As they were putting everything away, she said, "Thank you, kind sir."

He said, "Sophie," and he fell apart.

"Jim, what's wrong?" She held him, asking what had happened.

He said, "I can't bear the thought of Abby knowing I'm not her dad.

"Shh," Sophie said, "she knows you love her. She knows she is so loved by us. I think it will be a shock, and she might need some time to sort through it. Ultimately, she knows she is loved by you. You are her daddy. All she has to do is look at her baby pictures and videos, it's all over your face. You are a wonderful father, and you don't make a difference between the kids. This will be okay. We don't have to tell her till she asks, and if it's before she is eighteen, we don't have to tell her. Why don't we go chase each other around the bedroom?"

He said, "I like that plan." And they even took a nap. Three days later, as they put all the kids to bed, Abby came back out with a troubled look on her face. She was soon to turn sixteen, and she realized they were soon to have their sixteenth wedding anniversary.

She said, "Can we talk in your room?"

They both felt sick. "Of course," they said. She walked over to the chest of drawers and looked at the wedding pictures. Sophie's tummy was hidden.

Abby said, "Were you pregnant when you married, or am I adopted?" Before they could speak, she said, "I think I'm adopted. I have brown eyes."

"You are not adopted," Jim said. "Your father has brown eyes, but this heart has loved you since before you were born." They were all bawling their eyes out. Abby ran to his arms, and Sophie wrapped her arms around both of them.

She said, "Your daddy and I love you so very much."

"So I was in your tummy when you two married?"

"Yes," they both said. "Who and where is my real dad? Did he not want me?"

Sophie said, "He doesn't know about you."

"Why?"

"Let's sit down. This is a long story, and I'm going to take you all the way to the beginning. I'm not going to leave out anything. Your biological father was a wonderful man. But the one sitting beside you is the real deal. There's only one that tops him, and that's your heavenly Father." She told Abby everything. Then she said "I was devastated when I realized I was pregnant, but then I felt you move. I thought God has created life in me, and this life has a purpose and will change me for the better, and you certainly have."

"Mine too," Jim said.

And they both loved on her, and she said, "So the woman who tried to kill you was your first husband's girlfriend?"

"Yes, and her brother, and his friends. Yes, and she is still in prison. The others are out."

"Why is she still there?"

"She tried to take three lives that day."

"Daddy?"

"No. You and Gran."

"That's so terrible!"

"Yes, it is! Those people have destroyed their own lives because they hate me and blame me for something that wasn't my fault."

"Why were you arguing? Why was he trying to make you go with him when he already had a girlfriend?"

"He was going to force me to have an abortion, that's why I was screaming and fighting."

"Mama, thank you for giving me life and not aborting me. I've had a wonderful life."

"And you sure have made ours worth living," Sophie said.

"Amen," Jim said.

"You two are the best parents ever."

They both hugged her, thanked her, and said, "You've been a great kid who has made it easy on us. You are a huge help with the other three, and everyone else's."

"I love kids. I got that from both of you."

"Yes, you did."

Abby said, "You and Dad are going to be just like Gran and Granddad when you get older."

"We hope so," they both said at once. They chuckled and said, "They were two amazing gifts from God."

They all three snuggled a few minutes, and Abby Grace said, "I think I'm ready for bed."

They said, "I think we all are." They were all yawning. They got up off the sofa, Jim pulled them into a circle and prayed over them all and for a good night's sleep. Jim and Sophie were thrilled that Abby had taken the news so well and seemed to handle it all so well. They agreed she was very mature for her age and had learned a lot as she had ministered with them to so many families.

CHAPTER 55

Thursday morning, Connie called crying. "What's wrong?" Sophie asked.

"I think Jordan is having an affair."

"No!" Sophie said. "I can't believe that! He is crazy about you. You were all here two weeks ago, and I didn't feel or see anything other than he was tired. I remember hearing him say to Jim that work had been very hectic and stressful lately. Has he talked to you about it?"

"Yes. He said he is having to work extra because the last two employees have called in to work a lot and haven't been doing what they are supposed to. I went by there twice this week. He was supposed to be there and wasn't."

"Did you ask him about it?"

"I'm afraid to. I don't know if I can handle the answer." They were both bawling. Connie said, "He hasn't been intimate with me but twice in the last two and a half weeks. I was the one who made the first move. He doesn't love me anymore. I have to chase him down for a bye kiss in the mornings. He has to have someone else."

Sophie said, "Let's pray." And they did. Sophie prayed she was wrong and that whatever was going on, Father God would give her the strength to talk to him about it, that God would work a Romans 8:28, and they would have strength to work out with God's help, handle whatever needed to be worked out, that their love and marriage would be stronger than ever.

When she said *amen*, Connie said, "Thank you, my sweet sister. I feel like I can do this now."

"Let me know if you need to talk, cry, vent, or scream. We are in this together. You know we are going down to Macon in the morning for Saturday's family reunion at Uncle Randy's and Aunt Connie's. If you need me, we can stop, or if you two need us, we can go visit family next weekend. Jim's last workday was today. He is officially retired as of this afternoon, so if you need us, we are a phone call and four hours away."

"Thank you, Sophie. I feel so much better. Thank you for asking Father to give me strength. I know He will be with me. Whatever this battle is.

"Amen," Sophie said, "and I really have a gut feeling since we prayed that it is not what you suspect."

"I pray not."

"Call anytime, and I mean that. I'm here for you. If you want me to come now, I will."

"No, I'm gonna do this tonight."

"I will be praying, you are gonna be okay. I feel it."

"Okay, sis," Connie said. "I love you to the moon and back."

"Right back at you—always and forever."

"Amen," Connie said.

Later, Sophie and the kids met Jim in town for dinner. He had no idea they had a surprise retirement party planned. They parked by each other, and as they got out of the car, Jim said, "Wow! You guys look great, just like on Sunday mornings."

"Thank you, dear. We've not had many evenings out in a while."

He said, "I'm sorry. I will have to pay more attention to that."

As they walked in, someone said, "Right this way, sir. We have some larger tables in the back."

As he led them into the private dining room, clapping started, and everyone said "Congratulations!"

Jim was so surprised. "Wow," he said, "you all got me. I never had a clue. I wondered why the kids were so quiet."

"Bribery," Sophie said. They had the most wonderful evening. Speeches were made, handshakes, pats on the back, and hugs. It was a beautiful evening. Everyone was exhausted, almost all the kids slept on the way home. They all brushed their teeth and got to bed. They were leaving early. Sophie had heard nothing more from Connie, and had the feeling that everything was okay, that Father God had it, and all would be well. Connie had her friend Teresa watch the kids. Debbie had to move back to Douglasville to care for her mom. Chris relocated, and business was booming. She and Jordan usually got together with them once a month. They all usually got with Jim and Sophie every three months. Jordan had called and said he had to stay late again, so after she dropped off the kids, she went by his business. His truck was nowhere around. She was very upset.

She called his phone. He said, "Hey, sweetheart. Is everything okay?"

"No, it's not. If you are not home in thirty minutes, I won't be home when you get here."

She heard him saying "Connie" as she hit the off button. She wouldn't answer when he tried to call back. He was terrified.

He said, "Sergeant Wakefield. I've got to get back to my truck. I've got a family emergency." He was home in eighteen minutes and came running through the door. Connie stood up from his chair and had a very upset look on her face.

"What's wrong? Where are the kids?"

"Do you care?" she said.

He looked at her and thought, *What is going on?* "What do you mean do I care? Of course I care, Connie. What is wrong?" He had tears in his eyes, and so did she.

She said, "Jordan, are you having an affair?"

"What is wrong with you? No, I'm not doing that. I never have, and I never will."

He stepped forward. She was crying hard, and when he went to pull her in his arms, she jumped back and said, "Don't touch me! You haven't wanted to touch me in weeks."

He said, "That's not true at all!"

"Really?" she said. "Jordan, you have lied to me for weeks."

He said, "Connie, I have never lied to you."

"Yes, you have, a lot lately. You keep saying you are having to work over but you are not there, and your truck isn't there. You don't

163

pay me any attention. You have someone else, don't you? You don't love me anymore."

Jordan fell down on his knees in front of her and fell apart. He said, "Oh, God, help me here. Connie, you are so wonderful, and I love you so very much. I'm so sorry I didn't talk to you about this."

"What is going on, Jordan?"

He said, "We've got troubles with our company. I've been at the store parking lot with an undercover detective. One of our employees is robbing us blind, and he is selling drugs at the store. We are planning to make an arrest tomorrow. I didn't want to scare you or worry you."

She said, "You've not wanted to love me either."

He said, "I'm exhausted and overwhelmed. I'm so very sorry. I had no idea how I was hurting you."

Connie dropped to her knees and held him and said, "We are supposed to be one. We were till recently."

He said, "I was trying to protect you. Not shut you out." They both cried for several minutes.

He said, "Please forgive me." She kissed him and didn't stop.

An hour later he said, "Honey, where are our kids?"

"They are at Teresa's. I'd better fix my face and go get them."

He said, "Your face is beautiful."

She kissed him again and said, "Rest. I will be back." He was sound asleep when she got back. She told the kids, "Daddy is very tired and not feeling well," so they were very quiet, brushed their teeth, read the Bible, said their prayers, and went right to sleep. Connie set the alarm for forty-five minutes earlier. She would remind him why he wanted to be home more. They both slept very well.

CHAPTER 56

Off to Macon very early Friday morning, they got up at five o'clock. Kids were up at five forty-five. They were on the road by six five and stopped for breakfast at seven. They made a stop in Douglasville and visited Debbie and her sweet mama who was about to go see Jesus soon. They had picked up lunch for everyone and ate at Ms. Daily's house with everyone. Debbie walked her out and said, "Sophie, that's the biggest meal Mom has eaten in two weeks. I'm so glad you all came. I needed this visit, and Mom did too. Lunch was wonderful. You all be careful on the roads. Have a great and an enjoyable reunion." The kids loved the suite in Macon. It was a new hotel and was clean and comfortable. They were all well rested, and the weather was great. Sophie had heard from Connie and was so relieved that all was well. Sophie and Jim were almost to Atlanta on Monday after an amazing reunion, when her phone rang. Debbie was crying and said, "Mom just went to heaven."

They cried together, and Sophie said, "We will be there in thirty minutes. How's the rest of the family doing?"

She said, "We were all here, and still are. Tears all around. We all knew it was time, and all together."

"Have you all eaten lunch?"

"Yes," she said. "The church brought lunch and plenty of dessert, so if you guys are hungry, it's here."

"We may snack, it's not been long since we had lunch." They stayed a couple of hours, prayed, and headed home. "We will be back here Wednesday afternoon. We will go make reservations now, and we will stay in town a couple of days. I will see if Connie and Jordan can stay at the same place." It worked out, and Sophie got them suites on the same floor. They all had a great time with all the kids together. Sophie took all the kids to the park to run and play so they would be well-behaved at the viewing. They were. She took them quiet games to play in the kitchen since they would be there a long time. Abby, being the oldest, kept them quiet in the corner of the kitchen. They had two games going and were being well-behaved. Sophie came and gave her a break. Then the two of them walked them around outside, then back in to play more games. In about thirty minutes, Jim came and played with them all. Thirty minutes later, they were ready to leave. They had two sitters to watch then all the next day. They chose assuredly not to take them to the funeral. There was viewing from ten to noon. The funeral was at noon, with no graveside service. They went and picked up food and ate lunch at Debbie's. Then they all went to see her grave and flowers. They all joined hands and prayed. Debbie's brother and sister were staying the next week, possibly longer, to settle the estate. Debbie and Chris were settled in Douglasville. They planned to stay there. Sophie and Jim stayed with Connie and Jordan for two days.

They said, "We've got to get home." They went home Saturday, and Sunday morning, as they were driving to church, singing, "He's Got the Whole World in His Hands," Jim and Sophie were holding hands. Their hearts were overflowing as they looked back at their beautiful children's happy and healthy faces. They heard a small sound, then their SUV exploded into hundreds of pieces. In an instant, they were with Jesus and their loved ones in heaven. The fragrance and beauty of heaven was amazing. To walk and talk with Jesus and be hugged and welcomed by Him was incredible. Back on earth, Frieda heard from her brother saying, "They are no more. I destroyed them all in one blast. No survivors." She was overjoyed. She thought she had won, but in heaven, the Nelsons were all together again, having the time of their life with family, parents, grandparents. Sophie's mom was expecting when she died in the car crash. She hadn't told their families because she hadn't seen her doctor yet, so Sophie had a younger sister no one on earth knew about. She was excited to meet her. Heaven was beyond any of their imaginations.

But as it is written, Eye hath not seen, nor ear heard, neither have entered into the heart of man, the things which God hath prepared for them that love Him.

—1 Corinthians 2:9 KJV

For there are three who bear witness in heaven, the Father, the Word (Jesus) and the Holy Ghost (Spirit): and these three are one.

—1 John 5:7

For God so loved the world, that He gave His only begotten Son, that whosoever believeth in Him should not perish, but have everlasting life.

—John 3:16

For God did not send His Son into the world to condemn the world, but that the world through Him might be saved.

—John 3:17

AFTERWORD

I give all glory to God for the writing of this book. I was watching a love story on TV one night, and He (the Holy Spirit) spoke the title of this book to me and put an image in my mind of what the cover was to look like. I thank Him. He writes the story on my heart, and I type the words. My prayer is that as you read through the pages, you come into a deeper relationship with the Savior of the world, the Lord Jesus Christ, and realize His love is the real love story, that you are so loved and worthy to be loved by Him. He held you in the palm of His hand and created you to love and be loved. He kissed your little cheek and filled you with love and imagination, and this world may have been rough on you and may have tried to snuff out every gift your Father in heaven gave you. We have an enemy, Satan, who hates God and wants to destroy His children. Praise God we have a Savior who loves us all enough that He purchased healing for all of humanity with the stripes on His back that was broken open for me and you. No one else could carry our cross for *our sins* like Jesus Christ did. When we accept what He did for us on that cross, and let His blood cover and forgive our sins, we find freedom and peace. We realize if Jesus loved us enough to suffer that kind of humiliation and pain for us, He deserves our love and adoration.

Jesus stands with arms open wide.

You can experience a love, peace, and joy that's so beautiful and have everlasting life. What are you waiting for? Just say, "Jesus, I'm a sinner, and I need a Savior, please come into my heart and forgive me of my sins." He will, and He will write your name in the Lamb's Book of Life, and when you take your last breath here in this world, you will take the next one in heaven with Jesus and live in paradise with Him for all eternity. How can you pass up such a wonderful opportunity? Please don't. Just pray, and if I never meet you here, I will see you there.

Love in Christ Jesus always and forever,
Victoria

ABOUT THE AUTHOR

Victoria began a love story in her heart at age ten, never imagining that one day, she would pick up a pen, put it to paper, and write a love story. Now she's working on a seven-book series with the help of the love of her life. Come join her on her journey and read along with her.

CPSIA information can be obtained
at www.ICGtesting.com
Printed in the USA
JSHW030244230322
24154JS00001B/4